MW00399735

# THE POET

# THE POET

## Louisa Reid

doubleday

TRANSWORLD PUBLISHERS
Penguin Random House, One Embassy Gardens, 8 Viaduct Gardens,
London SW11 7BW
www.penguin.co.uk

Transworld is part of the Penguin Random House group of companies
whose addresses can be found at global.penguinrandomhouse.com

First published in Great Britain in 2022 by Doubleday
an imprint of Transworld Publishers

A CIP catalogue record for this book
is available from the British Library.

ISBN 9780857528391

Typeset in 10/13.75pt Sabon LT Std by
Palimpsest Book Production Ltd, Falkirk, Stirlingshire
Printed and bound in Great Britain by Clays Ltd, Elcograf S.p.A.

The authorized representative in the EEA is
Penguin Random House Ireland,
Morrison Chambers, 32 Nassau Street, Dublin D02 YH68.

Penguin Random House is committed to a sustainable
future for our business, our readers and our planet. This book
is made from Forest Stewardship Council® certified paper.

To all the women who want

If there is blood on the hearth who'll know it?
    Or blood on the stairs,
When a murder is over and done why show it?
    In Saturday Market nobody cares.

'SATURDAY MARKET', CHARLOTTE MEW

'Miss Mew is far and away the best living woman poet
– who will be read when others are forgotten.'

THOMAS HARDY

# MICHAELMAS TERM

# HUNGER

There are students everywhere:
strutting magpies,
they chatter in black gowns
and white bow ties –
crowds of them loudly matriculating.

I wait
and watch,
lean against a wall beneath the Bridge of Sighs,
wearing
a tight black dress
and stupid heels that trip me up
on the ancient stones.

I wonder if I laughed as much
when I was them
or smiled so widely,
can't remember where I went that day,
what I did, with whom, or why.

Smoking a cigarette, I stab the wall
with a stiletto
and wait for you
to come cycling up the lane, barrelling forwards,
the rebuke of your bell
the chiming tinnitus of evening.

I ought not to be here, wasting time,
should be inside one of those book-lined rooms,
safe in the refuge of paper and hard work.

I have been attending to other things.

In the last week I have noticed
the colour of turning leaves,
vivid shocks of sun slicing across crenellated skies,
and I have noticed the smell of the season,
damp and rich,
so dark it's almost black,
and the rub of soil in my shoes, between my toes.

I have been thinking about how things rot
and decompose,
wishing I understood the chemistry of it,
the biology and physics
of degeneration

so that I might apply this understanding to
loss
of my own.

Because if ideas can breathe
then surely they can lose the will to live.

⸕

'You shouldn't smoke,'
the man beside me says,
his spectacles skew-whiff,
breath hot with port,
ripe with cheese and opinion.

I've forgotten his name
and he won't know mine,
but he's someone I should be trying to impress,
gatekeeper,
keyholder,
big      swinging      intellect.

I should try at least to oil his hinges
with the grease of my servility.

I understand deference and
the imperative
to not embarrass you, or myself,
but tonight my head refuses to nod
and my smile is a dead thing.

I shrug and take out my lighter and a cigarette.
'Well, at least I'm still young enough to give up,'
I say, swinging my legs free from under the table.

Ignoring swivelling eyes and
looks exchanged –
like a congress of ominous old birds
they stare –
                    I walk away.

The candlelight shudders
and the faculty turn back
to peck at their cheese
and the state of the world,
of which I am an apposite example,
certain of their a priori assumptions
about my behaviour:

        young,
        too much lipstick
        and skin,
        silly, emotional,
        doesn't know what she thinks.

I don't excuse myself,
just stride away, out
and into the quad,
take off my gown
and breathe.

You follow me,

'What was that?'

I light the fag.

'What?'

'Do you have to be rude
to everyone you meet?'

I shrug.
'Do you really have to
patronize me?'

Once I would have been so grateful
for this privilege:
my place at the table of success
where brains are spread like butter, or –
for you – undergraduate legs.

'Why the hell did you want to come?'

'I didn't,' I lie.
'So, actually, Tom,
I'm going home.'

I could ask you to leave too,
but I won't.
It doesn't mean I don't want you to offer,
that I'm not waiting for you to bother with me.

This morning, running my hand
over your head, holding your jaw
to angle your face,
feeling for the brute force of your thoughts,
I wanted to
ask what you felt about us.
We kissed

and the mirror watched, making a marvel of you:
Rodin's beautiful thinking man incarnate,
my half-dressed body against your naked back,
an inkling of summer still on your skin,
as the bedroom and everywhere filled with our
    reflection.

You shake your head, a decisive *no*,
and look at me with the glance
you reserve for people who make your
stomach and eyes roll:

women waiting for buses
in short skirts, chewing gum,
with a racket of children who run under your bicycle
    wheels;
the thud of their footballs against ancient walls.

Or undergraduate work
that insults your brain –
the girl who left your college last year,
she was weak, you said
(in how many ways?),
and clearly never deserved her place.

I'd thought she was sweet,
nervous and sincere,
when she stood in the quad last autumn
hovering on the edge of a shadowy lawn.
A night like this
when soft lights twinkled
the grimace of gargoyles into a fairy tale.

It was supposed to be fun.
Your annual welcome to a new cohort of freshers,
an open-armed night profuse with champagne,
but I saw myself in the way she drank too fast

and in the way she jumped when you laughed,
looking over her shoulder,
straightening her clothes,

just in case she was the joke.


&

'Whatever, suit yourself,' I say,
'but don't wake me up –
I'm going straight to bed.'


&

You're home,
bloated with wine,
your bulk loud in the shadows,
and I have been sitting up
writing messages into the air
with the tips of my fingers and toes –
my body a nib
sharp and dark with the ink of waiting.

We collide in the kitchen,
jaws snapping
*Who? When? Why?*
*What's been happening?*

Evenings end up this way –
you push past,
rough, fast,
and leave me standing
mouth                    open
and
alone.

# THIRST

It rains all night.
Battered by the percussive thunder of your snores
and the storm outside,
I watch the sky
                    vomiting
                                fists
                                        of
                                            ice.

The garden is running with leaves,
the street awash with trash,
wild night unleashing wild things –
words
and meaning
untethered from ruled lines.

Standing in the kitchen, back door open wide,
surrounded by the clothes I haven't ironed,
yesterday's pots I haven't washed,
I let the rain come –
step into the puddles on the path.

Drenched, I open my mouth,
drink rain

and wait for
                what?

In the dark earth,
in the patch of ground
by the road,
by the tree,
I put my hands in the dirt and
shine my torch on tiny flowers,
*cyclamen*,
I planted yesterday,
folding my tongue around the word

until it became an incantation,
a spell for a storm
I knew was coming.

Why did I bother?
Perhaps it was just to spite myself,
to give me something else
to swear about,
another way
to force myself to begin again.

Maybe I just wanted to observe
suffering
and understand better
how indifference operates.

In the dark,
hair wet across my face,
I cradle limp, shredded leaves,
dirty my hands with soil
obliterate petals and
hold out my palms – filthy and cold.


## DAWNING

'God, look at this day –
have you seen the state of it?'
You pull up the blinds and stare outside,
stretch
and stop me,
hold me,
and as we watch the rain
I take your heat
and the thick sleepiness of your kiss
and am fluid beside you.

But your words
wonder if I have meddled with the sky
and am responsible
for the mood you have woken with,
the dark surge of
your stinking hangover
as bitter as the coffee you pour for yourself
when we go downstairs,
waking up slowly to each other,
remembering all the reasons
not to smile.

You grumble:
why was I so rude last night?

I hold the butter knife
tight in my fist and imagine
sticking it
somewhere

between
your ribs,
or into an eye.

But it is blunt
the edges rounded and the handle old,
ivory weakened from hot water and ill use:
your mother's cutlery,
which I have spoiled,
you said,
and should have cared for better.

I bit my tongue
didn't respond with the acid
I longed to throw,
didn't say
that by the time
I moved in
it was already tarnished.

I know that if I dared even try

                              to thrust or parry –
you would catch my wrist
and push me back against the counter-top,
enraged, or perhaps
only

bemused.

You would hold me up with your words
grind me
into a pulp
leave me rotten, sour:
spoiled fruit.

Instead I wipe up last night's spills,
scrub at the circles of red
that could be mistaken for our blood
but are only wine –
wine that splashed over the lip of a glass
when you pushed past as I poured.

You tutted when I swore –
'Fuck's sake,'
I said,
and you replied,

                              'Language, dear,'
in a voice that mocked, and meant

                              *I'm not sorry at all.*

What had we argued about?
What was the cause of our discontent?

I don't remember now,
rarely do,
easier to pretend you didn't hurt me
as I can't hurt you.

                    ∽

You retreat

out of the kitchen
into your study.

Because you are
*An Intellectual*
I mustn't disturb you
and the rattle of the door as it is shut
announces that
I must leave you with your pen
and papers and
books
and very important
thoughts.

I imagine you staring at the screen,
chewing at your fingers,
ripping them raw as you work,
and hear you begin to type
then scribble,
furious.
Huge shoulders tense and mouth tight,
you drill into the work
like a man fixing the road
boring trenches for pipes
laying down essential systems
maybe wires, or telephone lines

but failing to communicate anything
at all.

It's as if someone has
cast a spell on this house
where nothing takes root, nothing grows –
we are surrounded by things that don't work.

Did you think that life would always be easy for you?

I think I thought
you'd help me be
the person I dreamed
I am.

ཀྵ

You don't share your fear
of the blank page.
It is a threat you do not wish to publicize
but it is written all over you:
in an image so carefully curated
to mark out your difference from the kind of men
who shamble across the city,
egg yolk on their lapels, smelling
distinctly out of date.

You accentuate your face,
its sculpted planes,
in the way you shave your head and wear your clothes

and I wonder how many hours you spent
seeking this version of yourself –
Greek god turned gangster –
in trashy magazines, or Europe's marble halls?

You enjoy the surprise on
people's faces when you open your mouth
and gift them with the privilege of your tongue.

I used to long to stroke your neck,
your head,
feel the buzz against my cheek,
and when I did I rubbed my lips
against your skin
and told you you'd be good on telly,

made you laugh
when I said you'd make the perfect rogue.

But now I'm privy to
a catalogue of complaints about
the state of
everything,
and your habit of not noticing me
unless I goad you into spite or rage.

It seems it's only me who's noticed
your decline –
did anyone else see
your nerves rattling last night?

Perhaps I misread,
perhaps I only describe myself.

But I'm sure I saw you forget the grace.
*Benedictus
benedicat*,
you stood there – mouth codfish wide –
watching me.

Why would you care how
I behaved?
Not unless you were trying to sustain
some image of yourself that I was fraying.

I do not invade your privacy
or ask you to share anything at all,
although I know the fear well enough,
the turbulence of self-doubt,
how it feels to feel
like you've run
out
of words.

## BEGINNINGS

At the start –

five years ago –

when it happened
in your office

that intoxicating
thrust of knowledge,

you didn't guard your piles of paper then –
your work
pushed aside,
my arse on your desk
as the afternoon sun and your mouth
and teeth and hands
set my skin on fire.

It was all about fucking:
the pleasure principle
so much more interesting
than footnotes,
you said,
laughing at yourself
as you straightened the mess and then
turned back to me,
put your teeth to my shoulder,
raising blood.

I walked away, dazed,
mouth a strawberry blister,
face grated rough as a stubble field.

Our fantasies met and matched,
I thought.

Now I wonder if my body were paper
I'd catch your eye.

Perhaps you'd take a pen
and fill me with words,
then strike through my flesh –
scoring out the lines that no longer make
                                        sense
until you find an undiscovered lyric
on the curve of my neck
the back of my knees
under my chin

and write me new
with another beginning.


## PARSIMONY

A determined chill creeps up through the floorboards
and in through the gaps
in the doorframes,
the windows,
but we don't heat the house.

I stare at the unmade bed,
wrestle of sheets
and crumple of pillow –
memory of an angry sleep.

I could put it straight,
instead I dress myself in layers,
remember thermals and thick socks.
*Don't be pathetic*, you'd say
if I were to suggest turning on a radiator,
building a fire.

You do not feel the cold
but my hands are freezing,
red and chapped,
gardening, washing-up,
the angry rash that has tortured me all my life.
I sit on the bed,
laptop before me.

*I will write this morning.*

But when I try,
manuscripts like murder holes
scream retribution as
I press keys only to
unleash a trail of crowing consonants
that clatter and chatter, angry plosives biting back,
growling dogs guarding the space where
                                        nothing is.

I should smash the reflection that
hides in those margins,
that mocks me, and smirks:
*useless girl.*

There are spaces where
there should be words.

I google your name
and sit, watching you appear on my screen,
smiling
as you don't in real life –
generous, scholarly, kind.
Lists of your books,
publications,
events.
You schmooze at me from
a page that lists your accomplishments:

*Newsnight* appearances,
Radio 4.
I play a recording of a documentary,
watch you stroll through a gallery
with a young artist, then on to a beach.
You are attentive as she speaks,
so charming, so convincing.
I believe every word you say.

That was always my mistake.

I snap the laptop closed,
discard it on the bed and ignore its
lips pursed in silvery disapproval.

Downstairs you cough,
then I hear you, noisy on the phone,
and try to listen in –
who is it you're talking to now, and what about?
Echoes of you thrum through the ceiling.

I pull on more clothes, mummify myself.
You're just tight,
I decide,
would rather see me freeze
than waste any more time or money on us.

It's everywhere,
the evidence of atrophy:
the pile of junk you choose to drive
and this house,
the bedroom ceiling bruised with mould
and your slippers
splitting at the heel.

I preferred you
in proper shoes.

In fact,
I think I'd prefer it if you smelled of oil,
tarmac,
grease.
Anything would be better than the stink
of your
superiority.

I go downstairs,
leave you to it,
to whoever is making you laugh,
leave you to
that voice you use
when you're talking to anyone but me
or your mother
or your ex –

a woman you married, briefly,
then left.

I don't say goodbye,
grab my purse, a bag,
and slam the front door.


## PUSSY

I used to like your words,
used to lap at them
like a cat at a saucer of milk.
I used to stroke you and tell you
how clever you are,
make you purr
as you shut your eyes and stretched,
languid and replete
in the heat of my admiration.

It's been a while since
I leaned over your shoulder and murmured,
*Let me see*,
brushed your cheek with my own,
relished the stubble scratch,
knotted my fingers into your shirt
and enjoyed the heat between us:
your breath
on my neck.

The day is cold inside my clothes,
the sound of bells swings in the sky,
and I walk
in the rain,
over a bridge,
wind-driven towards town.

Cars smash puddles up and over pavements.
I breathe in exhaust fumes,
and that sleepless night
shadows me.
I rub my neck
and think about all the places I ache,
the places where you don't touch me.


## SIX YEARS AGO

Empty quad,
low-hanging clouds
threatened to split
and spit
down rain.

I didn't realize the clocks had changed.

The choice:
to sit on a bench and wait,
or walk through the mist
by the river,
lose myself there in the depths of the trees,
go back to a dark room,
narrow-windowed, up too many stairs,
and sit on the bed
cross-legged,
to stare in silence at the walls or
slide under my duvet and hide
from things I didn't understand.

I could read,
or write an essay that was due,
check my phone,
pretend not to count the seconds until it was time
for the drinks and the lunch
and the chat.

I sat at the table later,
mute
without the skill, the dexterity of tongue
to know how to speak to a professor –
ancient, white-haired –
whose specialism in politics and philosophy
rendered her
dignified and astute.
She examined us as we ate roast lamb,
chewing over ideas
and soft meat.

The girl beside me said
something clever about Schengen
and I didn't even know what that meant –
not in terms of facts and statistics at any rate.
I preferred poetry and stories,
could talk about borderlands

and distances, liminal spaces,
in-between places –
but I wasn't sure that was the point,
wasn't sure it was relevant
or how to start, to smooth a new conversational path
without confirming how different I was.

Estranged from
them
and from
myself,
I sat tasting nothing,
sipping water,
scratching.

Pale blue eyes
pierced my ignorance
when the professor asked me what I thought –
apparently she didn't realize
that my mind didn't work
like hers.

But then, when they looked at me –
the others –
with pity
but no surprise:
already I had been characterized
by my lack of sophistication
(I was ugly-vowelled
and too loud;
I needed to learn to pipe down),
I knew they thought
I didn't know how to talk their talk.

I decided not to care so much
and somehow something came out of my mouth
that sounded clever enough.

She nodded
as I bastardized Eliot –
and said that
exploring ends in cognizance;
that to arrive back at the beginning
is to find the meaning
that we might have originally missed.

I found one of my smiles,
a big one –
all teeth and pink cheeks.
I grinned and glugged the wine
and acted my way in.


## STUMPED

But I am always the girl
who doesn't know
quite the right answer.
Even now,
twenty-five
and fully grown,
fully woman,
I know the self that sat
alone that day,
awkward in that company,
still follows me, her doubt
as painful as a blister on the heel
or a broken toe,
hobbling me.

I have blagged my way through life
and am still afraid I don't get anything right.

The day doesn't get any brighter,
the clouds have sunk

and I walk with them
on my shoulders,
caped with new disappointment.
Nothing is open.

I wait outside the supermarket
breathing in second-hand cigarette smoke
then slide inside.
Squinting against the hard fluorescence of the lights,
I try to remember what I have come here for.

I pull things you like from the shelves
and focus on what I'll make for us to eat,
but none of it makes sense –
the eggs
don't match the fish
or the cheese
and I wonder if I'm choosing the wrong kind of wine.

I can hear you ask me why
I bought this, or that,
and it's a mess,
like me,
no style to my trainers
or lumberjack shirt several sizes too big,
hair tied in a knot on top of my head,
face chapped red by the wind.

No wonder
you aren't bothered
when I turn off the light
and roll over,
no wonder
you prefer the inner workings
of your own mind
and your side
of the bed
to mine.

But I don't want you to touch me now,
because I don't know where your hands have been,
and if the bed seems too big
then perhaps that is because I have shrunk
to fit the space,
            lost in the wasteland of what was.


## COLLISION

I see her at the last minute:
Margaret Browning
weighed down with bags – like me –
she waves
and I can't pretend I haven't seen.

'Get in,' she says,
'I'll give you a lift –
it's awfully cold, Emma –
that bloody wind
and you don't have a coat.'

I say, 'I'm fine,'
but she insists
so I sit
with my shopping on my knee,
shivering.

She doesn't ask about you.
I like pretending you don't exist
but when she asks about my thesis
I wish I could say something
that didn't expose
my inaction,
and inability to function.

'Look, why not present your research to date?
It might help you to make some more progress
and I'd love to hear about Charlotte Mew.
The more I read of her
the more I understand what drew you
to such a vital, inimitable spirit.
It'll be a treat for our undergrads, too.
How exciting, Emma. Onwards, yes?'

I cringe into my seat
but promise to be in touch
with a suggested title for a talk.

The very thought.

Home – I kick one door shut and
another open
and drop the shopping on to the floor,
burning up,
cold sweat pooling in the small of my back:
maybe I want a drink.

You shout,
'Coffee?'
and I stick the kettle on
and pull out what's left of last night's wine,
stare at the dregs,
put it back,
clatter two mugs from the cupboard,
making as much noise as I can –
banging and crashing,
filling and stirring,
the metal on china strike
that means you will have to notice me,
have to
appear out of your lair
and say something –

anything.

Touch my hand,
or my hair.

Help me to unpack the bags,
and thank me for the effort I've made.

Instead you barely look up when
I hand you the cup.

You murmur something which sounds like
*Fuck*
and score a line through your words,
lick your finger,
flip the page,
find a blank slate.


## TABULA RASA

I think that's what you thought I was.

I came from countryside,
from hills,
and from people who didn't read books,
you thought.

It was easy to come to the conclusion that
I was your Tess,
pure, simple girl,
and you were my Angel, of course.

I didn't say no,
well,
actually
I was just another girl

who'd been called odd at school
for liking books more than boys,
for preferring words to tongues or
intruding fingers,
and scorning small-town ideas about what I could become.

I didn't mention
a new estate
where all the roads were
named after birds
which no longer sang in our hedges and trees,
or that the hills were miles from where we lived.

You taught me the Victorians –
and Hardy's verse,
you said, far surpassed his other work.
I nodded and, trembling,
approached you after our seminar,
held out a sheaf of papers as if it were an apple,
wondered if you'd take a bite, read my words:

poems I'd spent hours with
when I could have been in the bar
making friends
or finding my way around this long-walled place.

'Interesting,' you said
a few weeks later,
handing back the pile of paper
that bore marks of your attention –
a question mark here; there an exclamation.

'Shows promise,' you said,
and I blushed
at the thought that I'd made
some sort of impression,
the slightest dent in the course of your day,

a fingerprint left,
marking a page.

I waited for you to notice me again.
It was hard to concentrate on the text
when you were there, frowning, waiting
for someone to offer an interpretation
of why Rossetti's
devotional verse
was so passionate, expressive.

Why was this woman so powerfully sensuous?

You looked at me like I ought to know.
I couldn't think: too busy staring at your
forearms, tanned, resting on hard thighs,
the seams of your shirt
where your shoulders strained,
your hair – buzzed short,
thuggish –
and a voice like cut glass
slicing into the silence.

I stared at your huge hands,
short fingernails that I could already feel
scraping my skin,
ragged with greed,
and watched your eyes slowly close in frustration
when no one spoke –
this lack of imagination
so utterly infuriating.

God, I stared – you must have seen –
how the way you wore your
brain on your sleeve,
the arrogance of knowledge
was what I wanted.

How puzzled you'd look
if someone didn't understand,
as if that was their fault,
not yours.

We hung on every word.

You were a celebrity, still are –
talking head
with opinions for rent.

Travelling to Manchester or London,
you leave me
counting down
hours alone.

We talked about you then
as if you were an Ubermensch;
awed teenagers
in a world red with ivy and
pale stone struck gold in the setting sun.

'He's so fucking fit,' the girl beside me said,
as we walked towards the porter's lodge,
wondering how you could be so handsome and so
    clever.
'I love the way he calls me Camilla.
The sexiness of that man's voice,
I bet he'd recite Keats when he was coming.'
We laughed, not realizing you were behind us.
You didn't care –
didn't pretend you hadn't heard –
just raised an eyebrow as you strode past.

Another night, not long after,
in the bar after formal hall,
some fancy dinner – famous guest speaker –
your bow tie already loose,

jacket off,
as if you would burst out of your suit,
the glamorous dramatist
on your arm.
I watched as you led her
into the mesh of student heat;
boys downing pints and loudly pontificating
on things they didn't know much about.
You looked as if you enjoyed the chaos,
indulgent, amused;
you bought round after round for me and the girls
and I nodded enthralled
as you talked about Beckett,
not understanding a word.

Tipsy, swaying towards you in my heels,
you caught me before I fell.
'All right?' you said, laughing,
and then you paused
and breathed in,

(your lips almost touching mine,
                    cheek so close to cheek),

you didn't say anything else,
just smiled as if you approved of something,
and I took this lingering,
this breathing,
as a sign.

# SIGNS

Can be confused with wonders.

❧

I stand behind your chair
in your study
in this tiny Oxford house
that is really too small
for two
but is where I joined you
after I graduated
and there was no longer anything to hide.

Being an Oxford don can add four years to your life –
I don't know what it's doing to mine.

I've stopped bringing up the subject of
Something Better –
a bigger place, maybe,
with a bit more room –
because I have no right to complain.

I don't have an income
and make no tangible contribution.

You've started to remind me
that I'm supposed to be working –
but these last few months
I've been waiting for inspiration,

and given up reading, lectures,
listening to anything more challenging than
musical theatre,
wearing ear plugs in the house so I can't hear you singing,
almost
given up on thinking.

33

'What is it?' you ask
not looking up
your eyes pinned to your screen.
I try to read what you're writing
but you minimize the page.

Last year I ripped up the new poems I'd written,
a collection I'd called
*Harpy*,
thinking that was clever,
pleased with my allusion
to rapacious women,
monstrous
and driven.

You told me it was clichéd.
I could do better,
should think again.

I filled a bag
with that shredded paper,
left the house
and tossed my manuscript in a bin.


## RUBBISH

I miss those poems I destroyed.
Some of them have stuck
to the inside of my brain
like the ooze of sap
trapped in knots and whorls of bark;
Calibans that cry out to me for freedom.

I recite the lines
when I'm feeling like maybe
I still have a chance,

that I'm not just a housekeeper,
a wife.

Except I'm not your wife.
Don't get the seal of approval –
the ring
the honeymoon
the baby

that crap.

I'm a lodger at best,
who doesn't pay any rent.
I'm a cook
and a cleaner,
barely a friend.
And you don't need me for sex.

I'm your groupie,
your cheer squad,
a poor hanger-on,
waiting to do
whatever you want.


**NOPE**

'Did feminism just pass you by?'
my best friend shrieks
when I call her to complain.

I'm in the garden
standing on the patch of lawn
behind the house,
where I am still trying to make things grow.
I prod a bed with my toe,
survey the devastation the storm has left.

You are inside
pacing.

'Women didn't fight for their rights
for centuries
and hand them to us
just for girls like you to give up.
You've had every opportunity
to do anything you liked.
And yes, you've made bad choices –
not that I'm saying I don't like Tom,
I do,
I can see what you saw in him,
I get the attraction –
but for God's sake, Em,
you've got to wake up.
If you're miserable, leave.
It's as simple as that.
Don't take any more shit.
Remember?
*Women in time to come will do much.*'

She quotes our old school motto
and I almost throw my phone
into the patch of nettles.

My mother enquires if you've proposed
when I call her next
to whine about
floors that won't stay clean,
food that won't cook itself.

I ask her what that has to do with anything,
tell her
that there's no achievement
in being someone's wife.

Miles of misunderstanding waver
between us
until she agrees.
'Sorry, love, I know you like your books;
I just don't want you to be alone,
you know, when you're old – left on the shelf.'

'Mother,' I say,
'I'm twenty-five.'

And a shelf of my own sounds fine.

So now I need to become
this stranger,
the woman I pretend I am.

        ~

I find a trowel and a spade,
its blade caked in filth,
clean it up as best I can, then start to dig.

The sun doesn't show up
and I'm glad of the cold
and the drizzle
as I work myself warm,
burrowing into the earth
and leaving behind the bulbs I have bought
that will, perhaps, in spring,
flourish, flower –
bold tulips, tiny narcissi.
I will wait for them to bud and
see what I can learn.

Soil showers my legs
and ankles,
creeps inside my trainers
and socks.

A jungle of weeds,
troublesome stalks of dry, dead things with
roots that twist and wind –
tough as hardened arteries.
Breathing heavily, I pause,
tired of the resistance,
wipe stinging sweat from my eyes.
There is too much to clear.

I stand straight,
stretch,
tip my face to swear at the sky.

You are laughing into your phone –
I watch you through the window
and want to throw something:
a brick, expletives,
just scream,
*What's so bloody funny, Tom?*
but I don't,
because you stop, look up –

see me and          smile,

and I feel you touch my cheek
with just that glance,
a bulb of heat
still there, buried deep, despite it all.


## IT WASN'T ILLEGAL

Not a sackable offence,
perhaps just questionable in terms of
morality or ethics.

You didn't teach me again
until third year
but I saw you here and there.

Once – in a pub –
I was all dressed up
in black tie (a borrowed fancy frock).

'Like a dog's dinner,' I said,
standing at the bar,
embarrassed, hot with the surprise of
having bumped into you when I wasn't prepared.
'Lucky dog,' you laughed,
before you turned away
back to your friends and conversation.

And then
the next day
a postcard in my pigeonhole –
unsigned,
but I knew your hand,

it crept inside my clothes
and touched me
with the words.

*Forgive me*, you wrote,
*What I meant to say was –*
*You are beautiful.*


## COURTED

You leave for a conference
at the end of the week
and I wonder who to call, who might want to
eat with me or stay up all night drinking.

In the end I make scrambled eggs,
sit in old pyjamas
watching the walls.

My phone buzzes and I jump,
knock my plate to the floor,
answer before you can hang up.

'Hello? Em? Are you there?'
                              'Yes, of course, it's me.'
'Good. Right. Well, just checking in.
How are things?'
                              'All good. I'm all right.'
'I'll be back tomorrow not too late,
perhaps we could go out?'
                              'A date?'
'Yes, if you like.'

This is how our love goes:
waves of interest rise, high tides crash
and I'm dragged back into deep water,
you swimming beside me, under me, over me,
and I'm buoyant with devotion.

                    ❧

Your key turns
and opens
                something closed.
I run down the stairs into your arms and
the smell of gunpowder,
whisky and trains.
You tell me of the fireworks
outside, ask if I've been watching
for you.
The house holds us.

You say I smell delicious
and that you like my dress;
you touch the fall and curve of it
at my waist, rest your palm against my back
on bare skin.
Later, you sit next to me
and our hands entwine
under the table
as you tap out messages with your fingertips,
walk them up to my wrists,
sparking nerves so I spit and hiss and fizz.
Your thigh presses closer
under cover of candlelight and
everything falls away, the other voices,
other people,
my reflection in the silverware a deeper red.

You write something on my hand
with your finger
and I try to decipher the message,
guess the poem you're giving me.
The game we play,
I'm slave to it, will wait, later
see if I can quote the right line,
find the sonnet
you inscribe
deep into my palm.

But you spot a new colleague
and beckon him over,
a young research fellow
who's full of enthusiasm for all things medieval.
He talks. You listen
and I try to calm my heat
as you shift away from me and towards him.

We end the night back at home, a crowd
of three, your voices opera loud.

I leave you talking and go up to bed.

∾

The front door slams and you come upstairs
and find me as if
everything is just as it always was.

I whisper the words into your kiss,
the words I've held ready,
waiting for you to tell me that yes, I am correct
as fourteen lines of our love are breathed
into our bed.
I guess,
'For as you were when first your eye I eyed?'
and you murmur,
'Yes, clever girl, of course – that's right.'

And we remember how to love each other better
in the dark.

## MONDAY MORNING

And off you go
on your bicycle,
leather satchel loaded with notes.

What will you teach them today,
those nervous undergrads
on the edge of their seats,
held hostage to your expectations?
I feel their relief when you
take off your glasses, and flicker a smile,
allow them a nod.

I lived for that nod for years –
perhaps I still do.

Am I still standing here
waiting for the nod from you?

If I followed you,
snuck into the lecture theatre
at the back,
would I fall in love
all over again?

It's an idea –
one of the better ones I've had.
Better than killing you.
Better than leaving you.
Better than burning your books
smashing your laptop
eating your words.

Because you are like nothing else
I've known before or since
and,
if I'm honest,

I'd do it all again.


## MAY DAY

Final exams loomed.
Smeared with quotations
and critical interpretations,
I slumped at my desk.
My best friend yawned, shook herself, said,
'Em, let's go.'
And so we stayed up to see the sun rise

and hear the choir sing
one last time.

Maryanne danced, high and ridiculous,
as I stood staring up at the sky,
still drunk and horny with tequila,
licking the salt from my lips,
listening to the dawn.
It sent a charge of something:
the sun breaking through the clouds,
and the voices,
sheer joy, sweet and soaring.

So when I turned around
and saw you by the bridge,
hands deep in your pockets,
face softer than I'd seen,
it sent me over to you, through the crowds and
the madrigals,
and you caught my smile
easily, caught the laughter,
the striding morning's sun.

It was like you'd been expecting me,
had been waiting all this time.
As the bells chimed,
you reached out
and took my hand –

or did I take yours?

Your thumb on my pulse,

feeling it surge.

## INCOGNITO

I've followed you before,
just to watch,
acting on a hunch
that there's someone, something, else.
And now I imagine wrapping my scarf around my face
and pushing my hair into a hat
and hurrying after you.

I wonder if you'd recognize me?

I shower, dress,
a swipe of red lipstick and I shut the door,
                              tell myself to get a hold
of these thoughts,
this sprouting paranoia
which is shooting its spores
into my chest
and mushrooming in the damp of my blood.

Out in the bright world I squint
but walk swiftly,
buy coffee,
a packet of cigarettes,
and wander through the alleys and streets
of a city pulsing with intelligence,
wondering what I did with mine.
I weave through Radcliffe Square
past students heading for libraries or lectures,
my footsteps a stuttering envious beat,
distinctly out of time.

I blow thoughts up into the sky,
smoke rings curl like questions
and I burn my tongue
on the excuses which aren't answers
to the question of why
I've failed.

*You're not writing,*
Maryanne said,
*and it's driving you mad*
*but there's still time.*

⮑

I haven't forgotten how to spend money
and am very good at buying
things I don't need
and won't use
with money I don't have,
money that I take from you.

I also know that you'd say
I'm a victim of capitalism
and intelligent enough to resist
pots full of thick creams
to dab under my eyes,
hiding shadows and signs that I can't sleep,
serums that will smooth my cheeks and
camouflage my fear.

I buy clothes that don't suit me
just because I like the promise of silk,
the assertion of leather,
and I see the woman who wears those things
walking paces ahead of me,
and imagine how much better I'd feel
about everything if only I could be her.

Every night when I could be reading
or writing
I fill virtual baskets with
intangible me
and pay
in ways I won't recognize.

Today I sit in the department store,
close my eyes and let
a woman touch my face,
make me up.

I know where I should be –
it nags at me
that my work
is waiting,
beckoning, whispering, complaining.
I hate that I'm overlooking my poet
who thought I'd come to claim her,
resurrect her from a tomb of obscurity,
make her relevant
and necessary.

The list of people I'm letting down
gets longer by the day
and starts and ends with
a dead poet
who would have killed to have
the chances I waste.

The make-up girl tells me how long my eyelashes are,
what beautiful skin I have,
such cheekbones.
I warm under her words,
this stranger makes me feel
like I haven't in a while.

I buy the cream, the concealer,
mascara, and walk away
already feeling
loss.

I could have married a local boy
and stayed up north,
suburban girl,
lived a life that would have been good enough.

I could have said no
when you came to my room
in third year,
looking dishevelled
and distraught –
when you said
that you thought
about me
all the time
and would I mind
if you stayed for a while?

I could have said no to the wine
and then to the kiss.
I could have said no to breaking the rules –

I made my choice. I chose this.


## DON'T LIE

I wouldn't.
I couldn't have resisted.
You were all I'd wanted.

I'd made sure you'd seen me kissing
other boys,
chose them carefully,
as if I could ignite jealousy,
heat its licking green tongue
when I lingered in the quad
at moments I knew you would walk by –
I could track you by the position of the sun in the sky –
knew that at the end of a long summer's day
if I waited
on dark forbidden grass
tangled with someone else
you'd have to notice.

Perhaps I tried too hard.

I thought it would increase my value
if you thought I was desired.

I'd ignored you
and then been extra nice,
worked myself worthy,
proved I had a voice.

I think attention was what I wanted.
I had to show
that I was better
than the others,
that I was special,
the most special
of all the special people.

How predictable.

And you were the thing,
the proof that I was worth
more than anyone might have originally thought –
that I deserved my place,
and had what it takes.

Polemical, political,
the papers courted your opinion,
retweeted your thoughts about
the pandemic of 1918
and how we could learn a thing or two
from history.

I cut out articles
and kept your tweets
saved in a folder
on my phone.

You made your name in the pages of
literary supplements,
in the broadsheets,
online,
ran Twitter wild,
found fame
in a world where no one gave a damn about
dead poets,

but you made them sexy and
I was obsessed,
tragically in your thrall –
rapt, you might say –
and now those other girls,
the ones I wanted to make jealous
and wonder what it was I had
that they didn't,
are making
six figures
travelling the world

and I am washing an academic's underwear.

❧

It is still cold
and the biting wind should send me home –
even the elements chide me,
spite me –
but I don't want to go back
and stare at the walls.

I walk to your college
watch for the deer in the park
then I turn around and walk away again,
only glimpsing through the arch
the lawns, the towers, the life
I want,

but I don't want it enough.
Not enough to push myself.

If I did, my own work would
have me in the library,
laptop bound,
writing up a thesis
that is now so late it might as well be
a museum piece.
I circle my poet, avoid her,
and she knows she's being ghosted,
poor Charlotte,
used to being overlooked and underrated.

I wonder if I met her in a college bar,
I'd buy her a drink
and we'd be friends or,
threatened by her intellect,
I'd designate her strange,
an oddity –

and laugh.


## DATE

A brisk Oxford Sunday,
when I was still a fresher and not yet
terribly smart.

March breezes stole my breath
as I cycled through town,
college scarf flying.

I was early and waited
outside white columns,
trying to remember all the clever things

I planned to say.

I'd done my homework
carefully.

'Hello,' you said
and I jumped.
You had the upper hand already
and made me blush
when you looked at me as if you knew
everything I'd been thinking.

We walked around the gallery.
Slow     paces,
                my      boots     struck     echoes
and I wondered
if you could interpret
the acoustics of my heart hammering
into the floor.

I thought
there was no way you could ignore
the fact that there was something between us,

as if looped around an
electrified piece of wire –
trying not to set off alarms
if we touched –
we trod carefully,
each perilous step risking revelation.

I couldn't speak.

(This was long before the kissing began,
before we had sex
within hearing of those old men
who build walls against obscurity
with collections of letters after their names

and papers in journals no one reads –
praying, before death, for a Nobel Prize.)

You were wearing trainers,
didn't make any effort to impress,
and looked as if you were on your way
to somewhere else
or had already been there – a busy man,
your day barely holding room for this.

You smelled of chlorine and salt
and I imagined you a bullet shooting
rocket-bodied through water,
half human, half mythology.

I didn't have the map to locate
the other world you inhabited,
didn't dare ask where
you planned on going next or
how you'd fill your time.
I didn't want to imagine you
in places I couldn't be.

I guessed you had only stopped off
to show me these paintings
as a brief duty call,
part of your mission
to educate the uneducated,
as if I didn't know what a museum was.
I played up to that,
wide-eyed and awed.

How had it come up?
We'd been talking Keats
and his Belle Dame.
We argued agency, and authority;
siren, or damsel in distress,
and you nodded when I said

that maybe it was just the fear of death –
death of the imagination,
death of the soul,
death of potential,
Keats failing to achieve
the only thing he wanted, the only thing we all wanted:

> to dream.


You'd looked at me longer than you ever looked at anyone
    else.


And then you mentioned the exhibition.


I guess the others presumed
they should get there under their own steam,
but I stood
in your red room
on the second floor
of your tower,
staring out of the window towards the
water meadow,
and asked you when,
what day, what time,
where?
You seemed
almost charmed by my guile
and answered,
'Oh, right, well, Sunday should be fine.'
But you were checking your watch


and when I leaned forward that morning
in the museum quiet,
reaching out to point at something,
a detail
that had caught my eye,
the shaft of light
in the bottom right-hand corner of a Holman Hunt,
surely there to symbolize

something important,
you almost wrestled me to the ground –

'Don't touch—' you gasped.

I stepped back.
'What?
I wasn't—'

My body flared blood,
a rash of embarrassment crawled up my veins.

'I'm sorry,' you said and
dropped my arm.
'Heavens – I thought – you might . . .
you know that the guard rail's there
so you don't touch the art?'

Laughter ratcheting from wall to wall,
chill echo of our nerves,
rising only to fall
into a prickle of heat in my face.

I rubbed the place you'd held me
and walked back towards the exit
feeling
      at an angle,
           acutely aware
                that any moment
                        I could slip
and slide into
           a glass cabinet
               and destroy some precious artefact

obliterate perfection
with my imperfect self.

❧

I've always been someone who fumbles things,
useless at catching balls and slow to make an idea form.

But I was fixed on you,
even if after that for a little while –
embarrassed,
ashamed –
I couldn't bear to see you
and missed two tutorials.

You left a note in my pigeonhole
that I read and folded
read and folded
read
and
folded
so many times that it began to dissolve –
*I hope you're all right*
was all it said.
*Do you need anything?*
*Can I help?*

I took it as another one of those signs.

&

Maryanne warned me not to fall for it:
the Lovelace schtick, as she called it.
I don't answer my phone
but stand watching traffic
and listen to her message that tells me
novels are to blame
for the things I think and feel,
and she's only half joking.

She doesn't know what it's like
to have been loved by you.

You text to tell me you won't be home.
I call and ask,
'Why?'
'Dinner,' you say.
'Well,' I answer, 'I'll come along.'
My stomach twists at the thought,
the treat again of eating food
someone else has cooked,
but you answer,
'No.'
And I wait for an explanation while you sigh
at my silence,
and say that it isn't convenient,
and that you have a late meeting,
and a later supervision
and there's no point,
I'll find it boring: you need to speak to
a fellow about some funding.

'I'm in town now,' I say.
'We could meet for lunch?
I'll get sandwiches, a picnic,
we can sit by the river, go out on a boat?'
I can see your face
as I say these words,
know that you will have barely heard.

Shivering in a meadow
is low on your list of things to do
today, or any day.

But once we kissed
in the University Parks
under the trees, in the shade,
our bodies marking the grass –
I wonder if I'd find our imprint still there
the shape of love

or if it has vanished,

as impermanent as the other impressions
I thought I'd made.

Your answer is short,
in tone and words,
'I'm busy –
as you should be –
look, I have to go.
Another day?'

There is always
another day – as if time will wait
for you to want me.

I walk towards Broad Street,
slide into the bookshop
and breathe in heat,
sidle down the stairs
to the shelves I come to visit.

It should be a place of prayer,
sanctuary,
but I swear under my breath
as parts of me begin to plummet,
stomach and
heart
sink
whilst my blood pressure rises
and my pulse
bangs
between my ears:
that heavy underwater thud, the drowning.

Scarf wrapped tight and high,
I let my eyes do the work,
let them search
for evidence that I'm still alive.

But there is no sign
of me here
on the shelf
where my book ought to sit.
I guess it's done – at last:
out of print.

&

That self, the woman whose name
adorned a book
at twenty-one –
she feels like a confidence trick,
as if I emerged for a while
like a rabbit pulled
out of a hat
and then
the conjurer decided to put me back.

It was one small book of poems.
A beginning, I thought,
not an end, like Charlotte's work,
which stopped short,
decades emptier for its loss.

I sit and nibble now on my thoughts
instead of turning them into words,
I stamp in my cage,
and stare out at the world,
waiting for someone to open the door.

Maybe I need to gnaw,
sharpen my teeth and bite
my way out
before I disappear for good.

&

I drop bits of myself
behind me as I walk home,
skin flakes into the cracks in the stone
and disappears.

I count my steps
walk in time to the voice in my head

that says I am nothing.
I     am     without

purpose, or place or brain.

～

I hate the silence of the house –
and returning less than I was when I set out.
Tomb-quiet rooms. Bone-painted walls.

I can smell drains
and half-dried clothes,
an infection of onions, mice and must.

I shower, change
and make myself up all over again.

Dusk falls
and the sky unravels huge and clear with winter.
It's better in the dark, this town –
colleges stark as cut-out castles
popping up
against the vastness of the night –
and easier to be lonely when no one can see
you cry.

I turn my back on the pockets of people,
student huddles, speeding bicycles,
groups of loud and lairy men

and girls wobbly in heels,
smoking, howling too loudly to convince
anyone they're entertained by anything
other than themselves.
I edge inside the bar and order wine
and sit alone and wait.

Someone always sits down.

I sip one cold glass of white,
think about the bottle
that I might have ordered,
but I don't want to look as if
I'm reliant, and besides
the wine is sharp and hurts my throat
when I swallow.

I haven't eaten much today
and that's another reason to be careful,
not to go too far, too fast,
not to risk getting drunk.

It doesn't take long –
here he comes.

Young,
they're always young,
my age,
so much younger than you, Tom,
and even though I am not afraid
of sitting in the light,
of showing myself
to strangers,
I am afraid
that I cannot conceal the truth from you,
that you will always see me
for what I am.

In some ways he's the opposite of you,
this lad,
but he's cocky too, smart, a townie, we'd say.
I wonder if I fancy him,
let him buy the next round
and chat me up
with no intention of letting him touch
even a moment of us.
But it makes me feel better,
makes me feel that later
if I wait up
in my make-up
I can tell you where I've been
and who with
and make you wonder
what happened next.

Maryanne would say it's worrying,
this need for
affirmation.

She would, right now,
point out to me how
unhealthy this is.
This need to hear some bloke
tell me that I've got great tits
and that he'd like to do things to me.

She'd be right,
of course –
it's pathetic,
but I don't mind
when the guy leans forward
and whispers
that we can go back to his.

The thought makes me sick –

we don't even kiss.
In fact, I draw back and say, thanks, but
I'm married and
I show him the ring
that I wear on occasions like this,
pathetic, fake, marital armour,
and I say I'm surprised he hadn't noticed,
that I'm just waiting for my husband.

He smiles, sort of,
and saunters off –
probably mouthing some
slur:
>            *Prick tease.*
>                        *Cunt.*

And I am not surprised that
I don't feel any better at all.

## STARVING

Turning the heating high,
I sit at the kitchen table
and eat chips.

Grease on my fingers,
I cram them in
and sip on a thimbleful of limoncello,
cold from the fridge.

It ought to taste of summer
but it strikes my tongue
like disinfectant
and I spit it out,
remembering Italy last August –

sweating in Portofino.
You scowled and said
the tourists bothered you
then urged us back to the hotel room.
We sat in air-conditioned dark
and I waited for you to say
that was it, enough.
Instead you left me on my own,
wandered back out into the light,
and I sat
drinking,
watching a storm –
gunshots of thunder and the sea
scorched with lightning;
the heat exploded
and rain pounded the waves.

You returned, drenched and sour,
strafed my skin with your tongue
boring bullet holes in my flesh.

I touch them now
my ears still ringing with the remembered
burn of your breath.

That week you complained about the beach,
sand in the sheets
and the sea – too loud.
I waited for you to go outside and stand on the shore
like King Canute
and tell the tide
to behave itself.

You didn't like
the sun,
the frigging doves
that cooed too loudly

in the hotel courtyard.
The smell of my sun cream made you sick
and I wondered if being
a prick was your way of telling me
our time was up.

I listen for the door
and eat,
stomach hot and full,
swelling up with reasons
not to speak to you.
I reply to the messages from my dad, my mum.
*Happy Birthday, love!*
*Hope you've had a lovely day!*
I tell them I'm busy celebrating
and will call tomorrow.

The only envelope on the table
bears the curves of your name
and I trace them
with the tip of my finger,
ink from your ex-wife's fountain pen:
Hannah would have known
what to say
if you'd dragged her to Rome,
she would have enjoyed travelling hours in the heat
on a dirty bus, then a train,
to see some painting.
Hannah would have appreciated
the Contarelli Chapel
and the mise en scène
whilst I searched for something to say
that would make me more interesting.

                                          ⟗

'You're still up.'
I don't look up from my screen.

I keep my eyes fixed instead
on the nothing in my lap.

You make as if to look

                          but I slam the lid shut

and you shrug and trudge upstairs
whilst I stare at the blank page
and press the space key
over    and    over    and    over    again.

The boiler shudders
and the floorboards creak
and the house
speaks to me of your whereabouts –

I track your movements and
see you standing, otter slick,
sluiced with water,
tall, wide,
hard thighs from all the cycling,
as you step out, begin to sing.

Perhaps you don't hate this.
Hate us.
Hate me.

Perhaps I've projected
all my misery.

                  ∽

'What were you working on?' you ask,
the question is innocuous in the dark,
'Your Mew? Have you made a start
on those final chapters, Em?'

'No. It was nothing.'
You can't see my face,
don't feel
my pain creep towards you across the bed.

Can I blame you for not hearing
what I want to say
if it's never said?
For not understanding how much it hurts,
when I can't tell you
what exactly that pain is?

You sigh and yawn, almost swallow me up
into the gap between us,
and then you're asleep
before I've had a chance to speak
and tell you that
I had an idea.

It might have been good.

You breathe and snore and fart.
Heavy
with the weight of
my eyelashes,
my fingernails and hair,
I gather myself out of bed,
slip towards the window
and the anxious moon.
She pulls me closer until I'm standing
with my cheek against the cold glass,
and wondering –
if my life were out there on the road,
disappearing ahead of me,
beckoning me after it, into the dark,
would I bother to run?

## WAXWORK

I write a poem, the first for weeks,
and before I can change my mind
I read it to you.

'Almost there,' you say, looking up.

I am sick of being modified
by *almost*,
sick of *perhaps*,
and being *nearly* adequate.

I don't know what it is that makes you hold out your hand
and take the page
and read again,
but you do.
You put on your glasses,
stare at me
and nod.

'You know, I think it's rather good.
This image here' –
you stab my page with a finger,
indexing success so that
I feel you touch her:

the woman I found standing before a fire –
sticky-gold and smooth; melting wax –

and the bear who, hungry,
spoons her up,

a breakfast

that solidifies in his throat.

## VACATION

Term's over for Christmas.
I wonder what you'll do
and don't mention your mother,
don't want to begin the usual discussion
of where we'll go.

Last year we drove
up the M6, and spent a day or two
with my folks. My dad didn't know
what to say to you
and my mother blushed
when you complimented her food.

For a long time I left you unintroduced.
Preferable to behave
as if I were an orphan,
someone without a past,
than to admit that I felt mediocre –
lower middle class.

You made a lot of noise in my parents' house
battling with the television to be heard.
Mum baulked and said, no, she didn't call me Emma
because of some Austen fetish,
and you winked at me
and I wondered:
was I supposed to be laughing with you
at my mum?

But you insisted on helping to make the gravy
and peeled the sprouts
and you remarked upon how clean everything was.

I took you to the pub –
hurried past the Christmas lights
and the pier,

the drunks and the litter,
the people spewing in the gutter –
to meet old friends
and heard my voice change,
that accent coming back,
the one I thought I'd lost.
You didn't take off your coat
and checked your watch,
spent a long time cleaning your glasses on your shirt
and pretending not to see my smile
that begged,
*Please, could you at least try?*

And then on the drive home you said,
'Now I know where you get it from.'

'What?' I asked.
'My smile, my wit?'

Slow smirk.
*Oh no, not quite.*

So it's your family's turn again this year
and I'd rather not
stay here alone.

I don't want to go there, either.

You are jolly,
singing in your baritone
the choirboy tunes of childhood.

(I snuck inside the chapel every Sunday for a term
to find you in your robes,
your voice deep and rich and loudest of all.

You would have made a hot priest,
although
you wouldn't have practised what you preached.)

I pack thick jumpers,
woolly socks,
and sit, scrolling for ever through the
messages on my phone
as we drive through the snow, in the dark,
down a long A road to nowhere.

I wonder who there is to tell
about this.

Earlier I said the weather was too bad,
made a case for why we should postpone,
sat on the stairs, already in my coat,
holding my bag,
staring up at you.

'We'll be fine,'
is all you said when I suggested
it wasn't safe to go,
not with the snow coming down thick.

Will no one speak all this way?

I break the silence
with a hammer.
A pickaxe on ice,
I crack
us open –

'Do you still love me?'

And hate the fact I've said that
and you've still said nothing.

But then you stop the car, flip the switch,
turn cold to heat as you reach out
to persuade me
that it's silly to think like that.

'Why be like this, Em?
It's you and me. Together. Yes?'
Your smile coaxes me out
of my hesitation and
taking me by the lapels of my coat you pull me close
and kiss the doubts
so their steam clouds the windows and evaporates.

❧

Your mother stands at the front door
watching us gather bags and coats out of the car.
I pull off my boots and leave them in the porch
and screw up my feet against the cold of the floor.

She greets you like the proverbial hero,
prodigal son –
Odysseus returning to welcoming shores.

She kisses me once.

Dry kiss,
cold lips,
a brush
of indifference against my cheek.

'I thought you might bring the children,'
she says, directing her words to you – the only
other parent in the room.
I flinch
as you tense and say,
'No, I did tell you, didn't I?
Hannah's taken them on holiday.
Skiing, it seemed nice
for them to go. I didn't want to spoil
their fun. Someone at least should have a good time.'

You laugh at a quip that everyone knows
isn't funny. It doesn't break the ice
that creaks beneath my feet now we're here
and everything's freezing over again
and I daren't step any further forward
for fear of slipping,
sliding invisibly into the
cold deep water that runs beneath every word
that is exchanged in this house –
every conversation an expedition into some Arctic region.

I don't mention our child
and how you've forgotten
the baby I lost.

A flood of blood and cramping pain
bring me back into my body,
the thud of reality,
and I make my escape, turn
and hurry away from Annette and her jibes
that find their mark over and over again.
No wonder I'm bleeding: punctured
and peppered with tiny arrows,
deflated.

Crouched over the toilet, I sit
and think about slipping away
through the plumbing,
wading through the shit
and swimming up to fresh air,
a stark cold field, bleak and barren,
far from here.

I shouldn't have come,
should have locked myself up
at home
and written all of this down.

# CHEAT

Hours spent in the college library,
lost in the carrels,
poring over obscure tomes,
I guarded my work from eyes
that were not interested in my disguise.

The shelves heaved words my way,
words that itched like skin, pages aged
and rotting, waiting for someone to read them.

'Is that you?' Maryanne said, prodding me,
and I nodded and dropped the act,
took off the hat,
the scarf,
and breathed in her smile.
'What are you up to?
Essay crisis?'
'Something like that,' I said,
slamming my book shut.

But when no one was watching
I snipped and snatched, stole and made
collages, patchwork quilts,
hybrid forms that began to breathe
as the images transformed beneath my fingertips,
and I read them through your eyes,
narrowed with suspicion,
I policed the pages
searching out infelicities of tone
anything that might incite derision.

Building poems like bodies as if I were Frankenstein's wife,
taking Plath's arm, Dickinson's tongue,
legs that belonged
to Stevenson, Rossetti,
I bled Moore's blood,

stole Adcock's heart,
set it beating into my work.

I typed up those monsters,
those crawling forms that
looked like poems
but were not.
Because poetry means creation and
I am no creator.

❧

You were the first to congratulate me.
The prize –
esteemed –
for poetry
was mine.

I'd fooled them all with my Trojan horse
built out of words.
All the old men who'd have to see
my poems in print, and then look at me,
peer through milky, hooded eyes
and think again.

How had they not noticed me come crawling in
to their hallowed halls?

I'd hidden myself,
mushroom quiet,
stealthy, discreet – and now
I wanted a revelation,
for them to
see my body in those pages,
find my mind and
decipher the code,
make an effort to know my words.

And then I wanted to scream,
*What, didn't you notice?*
*It's just plagiarism,*
*I'm a fraud, an imitation.*
Instead I took it all – the praise,
the admiration, let you
buy champagne
watched you shake it, then spray it,
showering me with your approbation.
Friends raised toasts, we spilled out of the pub
on to the street
and they threw their arms around my shoulders and
you whispered in my ear,

told me I was incredible, phenomenal;
*genius girl.*


I caught you with that lie –
the lie that I could write.

Hung it out,
a juicy maggot, invaginated worm,
squirming and turning
on the end of a line.

You put your lips to it:
gills open, sucking, breathing in.
I sank my hook into your cheek,
dragged you away from all your
should-have-beens
and made you stay in bed with me.

I have loved you best in that smudgy darkness,
our love scribbled on the sheets
and up the walls.
The generous tenderness of your hands.

You sitting, resting, head against a pillow,
as I talked nonsense and stories into your chest,
the conversation of your heartbeat.
A good listener, I thought.

❧

New College,
smoky November night,
published poet, shiny new graduate,
I climbed the stairs to a long, dark room,
lamplit, creaking
with people waiting to hear me read.

I'd swigged Rescue Remedy in the pub,
then a shot, and burning up
I regretted my jeans, pink fur coat, the tight top,
smelled myself, rank and strung
out, dripping fear. I slowed and froze.
'It's fine,' you said.
'Emma, you'll be wonderful.'

People turned to stare.
Strangers, expecting something.

I ran. You followed,
held my hair as I vomited on to the grass
and a porter tutted.

'OK,' you said.
'It's too much.'

You took me home and I crawled close,
burrowing under the sheets, away from myself.

❧

Your mother is in the kitchen
flanked by your aunts and your sisters,

every one of them an over-achiever:
QC, scientist, politician,
you now simply their baby brother.

They smile as you regale them
with stories about your class,
the one on Tennyson
where you beckon girls into gardens
sensuous and full
with the promise that they can be goddesses, too.

You mention the various publications
you will write for this year,
an interview with the *Sunday Times*,
a possible column in the *TLS*,
a TV slot
that's in the pipeline,
your brand-new blue tick on Twitter.

Your mother is nonplussed at the mention of that
and I feel like saying, 'Who gives a shit?'
Instead I smile and nod as
you list other triumphs,
tell them what they want to hear,
throwing out erudition
as if this is an audition for the part of the perfect son.

I don't take this opportunity to remind you that actually
you never call
and it is I who have bought your mother
the cashmere wrap,
it is I who packed the presents for your nephews and niece,
who remembered the cheese, the bottles of Sancerre,
and reminded you to send your children
cards and gifts two weeks ago.

Dereliction of duty, I could say.
But you'd argue you've been busy, and after all,

what else do I have to do?
*Because you're not working, Emma, are you?*

I linger at the edge of the room,
want to offer to help to peel, or chop or
stir, lend a hand somehow,
but no one seems to notice that I'm there.
I could wait for ever –
hang my heart out on a chain and
set it swinging in the breeze,
rattling at strangers strolling by.

I stand outside the back door
and light a cigarette
that crackles damply as flakes of snow fall
into my hands.
I think about how
I'm rusting,
the four chambers of my heart
thickening with waiting.

Back indoors
I'm loud –
deliberately so, demanding to know
what I can do.

You won't look up, but stuff your ears
with other sounds:
the pop of corks, the clatter of knives,
the fireside's roar,
here in the Old Vicarage
where your father once presided,
great philosopher and theologian.

Is it because I make too much noise
        – squeaking advertisement of desire –
that you have silenced me?

If I am quiet enough, then maybe I will hear
whispered words come calling
through the trees, the seas, crawling up out of my veins.

And when I am quiet enough, then perhaps you will notice
that I am here
and give me more space to breathe.

I wait for the moment when
I will unpen myself, spill free of my inky cage –
corset of pain –
and escape.

∽

Over dinner there is too much wine,
I drink fast
and spill sauce down my front,
keep quiet,
not speaking unless spoken to.

Eventually Annette says,
'So, Emma, are you writing again?'
I choke, potato
caught in my throat,
and shake my head wildly,
flapping my hands,
cough out a
'Shit, fuck, sorry' –
swallow half a glass of wine and deliver
my best fake smile.
'No. Still sponging off your son,
but you never know,
maybe this year I'll get back to it –
I want to finish my doctorate,
then publish again – my poetry –
hopefully,
if anyone will still print me.

I mean,
who the hell reads poems anyway?
Just fools like us, right, babe?'

You don't answer, blink, turn away

and then smile at the table and say,
'Actually, I have rather an exciting announcement to make.'

What? What is it you need to declare?
Your laugh is generous and the words are loud
as you tell us that you have
finalized your latest deal:
a book
on what has so often been misunderstood –
the poetics of gay women and
their enduring invisibility within the canon.

Since when did you care?
What the hell would you know?

'Oh,' I say
but no one hears me complain that
I don't understand why this is news
to me
or that this seems to be a surprising direction
for you.

'Oh, well done, Thomas.'
Annette kisses you,
flushed and pleased, as awed by your
achievements
as if you are still her little chorister
shattering C sharp.

'Why the hell didn't you say something?'
I demand,
but you

begin another conversation
in which I am not invited to participate.
I'm expected to raise a glass to you, all the same.

In bed, chilly, aloof, you turn your back.
'Why did you make a scene?' you ask
and I wonder what you mean.
Did I drink too much? Probably.
Of course I must have been
inappropriate.

Perhaps it's because I questioned your motives.

The first time I stayed here
your mother put us in separate beds.
You didn't demur
when she put me in my place.
My room was narrow,
the bed hard,
the sheets smelled as if someone else
had slept there.
Perhaps it was just the dog.

I slept in my clothes
on top of the duvet
until you came and found me,
held my hand and led me
down the dark corridor
that creaked with our impatience
to be together.

Tonight I slide under the sheet,
naked
and prepared to use
my body to get what I want.

The sex is dry although the sheets are damp.
You scrape against me

and I can smell the house
groaning, smoky.
Your feet are cold
and your breath is garlic and deep red wine.
I put my mouth on yours and bite your lips,
think of vampires, succubi.

&#x223D;

Church bells announce the day
and I wait for you to open your eyes
before I get up.
I want to talk to you about your book
but you roll over when I say your name
and cover your eyes with your arm.

Downstairs your mother is making tea:
she warms the pot,
fills it with leaves and hot water
then looks up at me.
'Happy Christmas,' I say,
but she shakes her head –
'Not really, not for me.'

We sit down at the kitchen table
and she pours a pale, thin stream into a china mug
and disappears into the steam.
I sip,
burn my tongue and then say,
'I'm sorry.'
(For what?
For everything she thinks that I have done?)
'Bit late for that,' she answers
and I want to ask her about the apportioning of blame –
the way she has doled out
sinfulness –
how in her eyes it is all down to me,
as if I'm some ridiculous femme fatale.

I want to remind her that Tom has a mind of his own.
He left his wife and children.
Not me.


Later we go to church,
drink,
eat turkey.
It's dry and I wash it down with even more wine.
Annette loves her gift, I think,
and she stiffly nods at me
as if to acknowledge something.


'What did you buy for Emma?' a sister enquires
and when you say,
'We don't do presents, isn't that right?'
I concur because it's easier than
making another so-called scene,
easier than crying
and easier than the first year here
when I made you a stocking that the others
stared at, before they laughed at you, and then at me.
Annette sniffed and said her son
wasn't a child.


It would be petty to demand
a gift; to expect one would be worse:
foolish. But my eyes fill
and I try to disguise the tears, by turning my head,
swiping at my face with my sleeve.


Full of food and bonhomie,
you look at me
as if you're trying to read my thoughts.
You used to look at me like this before
and I catch sight of an emotion I've been longing for –
a softening
that speaks of empathy and understanding –

but it doesn't wait
and your face resumes its indifference.
I can hear you tell me
I've performed yet another misreading.

'You don't mind, do you, Em?'
You pat my knee as you're filling your glass
and don't ask me if I'd like another drink.

Sometimes I think if I waited for you
to offer me
sustenance
I'd
starve.

'It's fine,' I tell you and pull away,
disappear outside to smoke
and wish that I could take a train back home,
sit on my own or break my spade on the iron earth
rather than play endless games with your niece,
who seems used to being ignored.

I stub out my cigarette and call inside for Lottie
who jumps up, pulls on her coat
and runs to join me
as the fat sky pelts us with snow;
we lie side by side,
make angels of ourselves,
eat the flakes as they fall.

Bringing it inside in handfuls,
I make cones out of cardboard
ransack a cupboard for colouring
and we turn ice pink,
green,
blue,
hand out the treat.
Laughing as it melts in the heat,

we eat, and turn our faces
into frozen rainbows.

⌐

'What are you doing?'
You've followed me upstairs.
I hold up the book I'm reading
that I haven't made sense of yet,
the words dancing, jigging
reeling
a churning incoherence of feeling.

You touch my arm.
'Are you OK?'

You lie beside me on the bed,
put an arm around my waist,
move close.
I drop the book, lose my page,
let you lift my hair and kiss my neck.
'I'm sorry about my family,' you say.
I know it's because you're drunk,
because we're far away from home and
the book you're writing,
the one that you haven't mentioned
and that makes you swear,

but this love
is better than nothing.

## VISITING HOURS

You don't want to go
and I almost have to force your arms into your coat.
Everyone else is ready, waiting on the drive
in the snow.

We walk the back way to the nursing home
through the woods,
to where your father, perhaps,
awaits his family.

Others are out
on Boxing Day expeditions
in red wellington boots, duffel coats,
cheerful scarves and arms full of snow.
They call festive *hellos*
that your mother ignores
and which I return
in contravention of some unwritten code
that says this day must be met
with silent contemplation of the fact
that your father is
in your mother's words:

*Done for.*

I wait outside.
Don't go in,
don't want to smell
boiled cabbage, piss,
don't want to watch your face fall
as he doesn't recognize you, after all.

His hands, last time we came, were so thin,
the paper skin
torn in places
and the nails grown too long,
something unmentionable under them –

and although I never knew him
beyond a brusque hello,
I didn't want to think that someone
had dealt roughly with this old man
who'd once dealt roughly with his own son,

but even so
in old age, when he'd lost his mind,
didn't deserve to be treated with unkindness.


I hope he'll remember you.
I pray he'll say, *Tom, Thomas, my son*,
and manage a smile.
I doubt it.
According to your mother, it's been a while.


'You should visit more, Thomas,'
she said this morning
and your face fell into stone:
you're so good at ignoring
anything that cuts too close.
And here we have the deepest wound.


They aren't inside for long
and I've kept warm
chasing Lottie round the grounds,
her long red hair
a blazing flag of fun.
She holds my hand as we walk back
and I promise we'll build a snowman that afternoon.


## NEW YEAR

I stand in Tesco's
staring at the things I could buy
to make us feel better for a while
and decide that
this would be a good time
to think of metaphors
for ending a relationship.

I get stuck before I even start on
break
up

and it's an axe,
the fear of being
split like that,
sheared
in two
like a plank of wood
bent and cracked over a knee.

The bottle drops and shatters,
spurting, sadly, over my jeans and shoes,
and I stand in the puddle of wine.

But we have guests
due to arrive in a couple of hours.
Your friends –
people who I am not looking forward to seeing.
Why should I be?
They're nothing to do with me,
but even so I don't want them to know
quite how bad things are.

So I clean myself up,
straighten my hair and
paint the heart out of my face,
pin back my feelings,
staple them behind my ears.
Hate this plucked and staged dishonesty.

❧

The satisfaction of dainty food – homemade –
every hors d'oeuvre a work of art,
a table laid with crisp linen
and flowers in bowls,

fridge resplendent, gold with wine,
and glasses shining,
the room bewitched by candlelight.

The reality doesn't match
the ideal I had.

I swipe at dust that settles somewhere else,
set out bowls of crisps
and nuts.
You take a handful
as you pass.
You've had a wash, clean shirt, smell nice –
who is it you're out to impress?
You fill your face,
new beard pebble-dashed with crumbs.
'Wine?' you ask.
'In the fridge,' I say.
You pour yourself a glass
and I try not to snarl when you tell me
you've invited some extras.

I nearly choke
as I swallow a response
as dry as the wine I'm not drinking.

My stomach rolls with unspoken things
that repeat on me
and wake me up in the night
with a burning chest,
tight with arguments we never have.

You walk away, throw words at me,
second thoughts,
'Just students, some bright sparks –
post-grads, mostly,
I told them all

to bring something to drink.
It's New Year. The more the merrier, yes?'

⟨ornament⟩

I skulk on the edges of the party,
know how to minimize myself,
merge with the books and pale walls
and your music
in nondescript clothes,
determined not to show anyone up.

What's the point in starting a fight?

Glass of wine in my hand,
the bottle at my side,
I'm determined to drink my way
into the New Year
with a smile that doesn't show
my insides.

I have them ready,
those smiles –
like cutlery,
I bring out the correct implement,
ladle out niceness,
disguise discontent with a spoonful of sugar.

The students are beautiful
and I understand
why you want them here:
you want their potential,
their promise,
their praise, and as if on cue,
you raise a topic that I'd avoid.

But the acolytes gather and nod
as you complain
about the girl who left last year:

another reason why
it is imperative you publish something soon,
to ensure everyone forgets
whatever it was she said.

You remind the group
that you never stepped out of line –
and to characterize you as a bully is grossly unjust.

You stir sympathy
and they concur,
agree that above all
you are fair,
a hard taskmaster, of course –
but this is the best of the best, right?

Listening to you defend yourself
I think
that's true:

how you make people feel is bigger than
bullied,
                    it's belittled,
                                        and broken,
a carapace crushed underfoot.

The noise grows, and voices lift to complain
and laugh
about students
who can't take the pace.
We all understand the implication:
that you only have time for the
crème de la crème.

You feed your fantasy
by gathering these sycophants close;
a canvas
where you draw a portrait that has not yet begun to
distort.

But who am I to talk?

My smile is a rictus grin
that makes
my cheeks ache
but I don't know
how to wipe it clean.

Was there strychnine in my tea?

It's too hot.
I go outside
stand by the back door and smoke
and think about that –
poison and such –
when a voice comes peering at me
through the cold.
'Hey,
how's it going?
Can I bum a cig?
You look familiar,
we've met before, I think?'

'Oh, no,' I answer slowly
into the dark,
'I'm Nobody.
Who are you?
Are you Nobody too?'

For a second there's silence and then
this stranger laughs, and I join in,
glad there is someone else here
who understands invisibility.

If not, then I'm the fool again and I stop –
cough and clear my throat.
Just be normal, I think,
for once in your life.
How hard can it be?

'Actually,' I say,
'I'm Emma – I live here
and I don't think we've met.
I expect he didn't mention
he has a girlfriend, right?'

You used to introduce me as
your partner –
the poet
Emma Eliot.

I don't know which one of those words pleased me most –

that I was yours,
or that I wrote.

It is nice to be smiled at under the stars
by someone
who wants nothing from me,
but I wait for him to slide away,
back indoors.
I don't expect he expected
to get caught
in a conversation
on a step in a garden paralysed
with snow
with a woman
who was a poet, once.

He only wanted a cigarette.

I fill his glass from the bottle by my side
while I keep talking,
so he can't answer the question.

I suppose I'm flirting,
easier out here to perform
the theatre of it
where he can't see the fraying

mouth slightly apart, the costume of tits and teeth
and smiley eyes, the stupid laugh
muted in the solid dark.
I hate that I know this part so well.

But if you don't want me,
well, maybe someone else will.
And if you notice he does –
will it remind you of what we had?

'You're not an undergrad, are you?'
I consider him, give him grateful attention.
His answer comes fast,
'Nope. I'm halfway through my DPhil –
the prof supervises me –
I'm Ari – Ariel,
I expect he didn't mention me either, though.'

He nods back inside the house, in your direction and
I ignore the look on this Ariel's face,
the hope that you might have
brought him up in conversation,
might have mentioned him
maybe once or twice.

It reminds me:
I'm not the only one.

I let my lip curl,
the merest hint of disdain
an attempt to lessen your power and
weaken your hold.
I lean in, touch Ariel's hand and say,
'Well no – but he's not actually a professor,
at least, he wasn't the last time I checked.'

'Whatever, he gets my vote,
the man's a legend, no?'

I change tack, I'm not going to stand here
and talk about you.
Blowing out
questions with the cigarette smoke, I ask,
'So are you nearly done?
With writing up?'

'God, no, barely started.
How about you? What are you
working on?'

Then Ari stops, checks himself.
'Shit – I know,
you're a poet.
The prof mentioned it, I think.
You won a prize, right?'

I tell him it's been a while since
that first collection,
mutter something indecipherable about
my research –
my poet,
her name: Charlotte Mew,
the thesis I ought to have finished long ago.

I don't choose to confess that
I've left my own poetry and
my poor Charlotte suspended
in files.

I don't explain
how my words
click
like slow clocks,
embarrassing in their brokenness.

I should tell Ari that I'm stuck
and that I've totally screwed it up,
but I can't.

So I fill in the gaps with
half-truths to disguise how I feel like
a joke that I'm playing on myself,
and as we wander back inside

I'm waiting for this man to explain that
I must have peaked too soon,
the best behind at twenty-one –
the wasteland of the future, the worst to come.

But there's no eye roll, or sneer, or condescending look,
just a nod, a smile
and his voice telling me
that he'd love to read my work.

I blush fast and hard,
oven hot, intense with the desire to
prove myself.

I could show him my book
even though he might hate it,
hate me,
afterwards, later
when he's seen all there is and wondered
what the fuss was.
Reckless, my mouth runs on,
pulling the rest of me behind.

'Upstairs,' I say, 'it's upstairs,
no room down here' –

I gesture at the walls
laden with the texts
you keep close –

'I'll run and get it,
if you want.'

Why did I say that?
How desperate
I must be
to impose
myself on this stranger –
what does it matter what he thinks of me?

But he knows my name
and that must mean something.

Ariel is chivalrous, so beautifully brought up,
topping up my glass as he talks, telling me
he doesn't want to put me out.
'I'll dash and grab it, just tell me where to look.'

～

Before we can decide
who's leading who
you interrupt,
your arm flung fast
over the shoulder of my new friend.
'I see you've met the great Emma Eliot,
Ariel, wonderful, well –
we were just talking over here
about—'
You start to lead him away,
gesturing towards the group who wait
and watch,
but I cut you off.

'Actually I was just about to show
Ari upstairs.'
The sudden confusion on your face,
the implication that we are going to bed
that I'm going to shag him
with you downstairs,
makes me speak too fast as

I take Ariel's arm,
the one that hasn't been commandeered
by your weight, and
draw him my way.

He comes easily, lightly, and
I suppose you daren't detain him,
daren't turn this into a tug of war –
how absurd that would be
in front of all these people:
bad enough they see me at all.

We climb the stairs.
I say that Ariel is a nice name.
He tells me it's a *Tempest* thing,
that his mother acts,
that they gave him shit at school
and it's not actually that cool, not really,
to be named after some weird magic sprite.
I look at him over my shoulder
on the steep narrow stairs
and his wide eyes
meet mine.

I don't believe him.
No one's ever taken the piss
out of this man.
He speaks the way someone talks
when they've never had to worry
about being laughed at.

It's a voice I hear all the time:
cultured, a drawl,
melodiously urbane, imbued
with prestige, but in Ariel
somehow still sort of street.
Like you, he's made a study
of how to make privilege hot.

So I keep my mouth shut,
fool myself that he is
more like me
than he would ever want.

I want him to know
where I'm from,
all the while
hoping I pass
as someone who maybe went to St Paul's too,
who likes boats
and fresh air,
was rowing at Henley before I could talk,
sucking up opera at Glyndebourne
as if it were mother's milk.

We are too old to care
about these things –
where we grew up,
who we know –
but already I almost see
that Ariel's past is so far from mine
that we will always be strangers.

I show him the spare room
full of boxes
and an unmade bed.
My things are flung across the covers –
piles of wasteful clothes
a nest of outfits:
women who I sometimes like
to burrow inside,
cocoons,
glittering skins,
now dried out and discarded –
I have slithered from body to body
in search of some elusive          self.

(As a little girl I liked to dress up,
tiny feet slopping in huge heels,
teetering in my mother's things.
She'd laugh and say
I was beautiful, perfection,
and I took for granted that it was true –
I thought everyone would always think so.)

I scan the shelves to find my book
and pray the words have not dissolved,
the letters haven't fled,
little gingerbread girls
frightened by hungry wolves,
scarpering in fear of dismemberment.

'It's not here,' I tell him,
shutting my eyes,
holding on to a shelf
with my fingertips
still just about upright.

I imagine you, Tom,
taking it
eating it
belching it into the city's fumes
farting it into the stratosphere –
my waste of time.
Or just squatting and
shitting it, flushing
and wiping yourself clean.

I imagine an exorcism –
you, the priest,
casting out the spirits
who have inhabited these books.

'Hang on, let's see.'
Ariel is bending at the knees,

scouring the lower shelves
where I know it cannot possibly be
because
I did not put it there.
I left it here
next to Emily Brontë,
Maya Angelou, Sylvia Plath
and Anne Sexton.
Friends who understand
what I might mean.

I look again. Last look,
I promise myself,
thinking it must be for the best
this disappearance –
a kidnapping, perhaps
an abduction,
or better yet, she's absconded
and is free.

Then I see it,
eyes finally focusing
as the room slips out of distortion
and I wonder how much I must have drunk
to miss what was right in front of me,
the shock of seeing myself
and the stranger I have become.

'Here!' I hold it out to him,
this bit of my life,
and wonder why
I am not hiding from this man.

Do I just want him to admire
the cover, my name embossed there?
Am I simply trying to impress with the words
on the back,
the names that said

that this is good, maybe even the best
new voice to come from my generation –
rebellious, lyrical and outspoken?

Maybe I don't even want him to look inside,
perhaps I'd rather he just
undressed me.
Perhaps I really did bring him up here
for that.

But I know that what I really want
is to be wished for,
listed – if not your number one,
then at least in your top ten.

        ❧

Later when we are counting down
the seconds
I catch your eye.
You look at me
as if you know
exactly what I've been doing.

I don't like that presumption –
that you can read me
and that everything I ever do
will be a mistake.

I smile and pretend not to read you in return as
you make your way across the room
in seconds, air-kissing as you go,
wishing everyone happiness,
your learned largesse
another sign;
you take in your stride this
shrinking house and all it contains
and tap your glass to mine

in a perfunctory salute,
a half-felt wish
of something good.

'Happy New Year, darling.'
I kiss your cheek,
and then your hand is already reaching
out to see
what it is
that Ariel clutches
in his.

You laugh.
'Good Lord, Ari,
I thought she'd taken you
on a tour of the etchings,
not to give you this.'

I bristle,
hear how you spit
on *this*,
as if *this*
is ridiculous, risible,
and I too am despicable.

You frown at me, playful,
as if I've been naughty, transgressed,
I'm waiting for your finger to wag
as if to say,
'Don't inflict yourself
on our guests.'


## JANUARY

New Year's Day.
You light a fire
and make me a drink –

it feels odd,
but I don't complain:
resolutions postponed.

I sip the gin, sink into the blanket
on the settee
feel almost fine, falling for the cliché
that everything will be better now last year is behind us.
Twelve months ago
I slumped outside into the white winter dawn,
my bare feet a depression on the frostbitten grass
my finger bleeding in the white of morning.
I had no memory
of gouging out a chunk of flesh
but sucked on iron,
the taste of my life then, after that death:
a baby, not planned, resented,
then lost.

You followed me outside with a blanket
and hot tea.
*Come inside*, you whispered,
a kiss on my forehead
and the kindness of your hand
on my shoulder.
You drew me a hot bath and then
when I came downstairs again you
read aloud until I slept, lulled out of fear
by the sounds of all the things I loved.

We sit
hungover.

You read on your chair
and I try to concentrate,
distracted by the speed and swoop of turning pages,
your eyes darting up to my face.

I recognize the key of your music,
its D minor strains,
and am about to ask you to tell me the story
of Mozart and this requiem
when you drop the book to the floor,
hard,
so the spine cracks –
and start.

'So. No apology, then? No comment to make?'

'Sorry? About what?'

A shout of laughter, you gesture
as if it should be self-evident
and I am so slow,
remedial, almost:
'Last night.'

You pause.
I shake my head
and you throw up your hands,
'You embarrassed me, Emma –
and embarrassed yourself,
behaving like that with one of my post-grads –
come on, you may as well have pulled down your pants
and pissed yourself right there on the living-room floor.
I thought you had a shred more self-respect.'

It's a slap,
a punch
so cruel that I'm not sure I've heard correctly.
'Tom?
I'm sorry, what?'

You repeat yourself, accuse me of making
one of my scenes,
and I

stutter out an answer that feels
like a non sequitur
but these are the only words
I have:
'I've been thinking we should break up this year.'

You raise an eyebrow, perfectly calm,
and nod, roll your shoulders, inhale.
'I see, this year.'
There's a pause, and then,
'When?
This month or
maybe February? June?
When this year did you think you might fit that in?
If you let me know then I'll make a note.'

Turning so you can't see my face,
I say,
'I don't know, whenever you like,
why not now?
You hate me anyway.'

'Emma. Really.
What have I ever done to suggest that?
Don't you think you're being a little extreme?'

The room is small
squeezing my lungs
snatching my breath
and you are huge
monstrous in your mockery
your derision –

*I am sure you hate me.*

I say it again
and now you laugh, speak softly.
'Don't be so ridiculous.

What is there to hate?
Please stop inventing
feelings for me which I don't have.
Last night was bad enough.
I'll have to call Ariel and apologize;
you can speak to him, too.
He was awfully good with you,
awfully polite.'

I can't even stand up
will not give you the chance to let your eyes
roam,
to look at my body
dressed in scruffy shapeless things,
will not let you sneer at my naked feet,
my bony wrists
and chest,
dismiss me entirely
with a glance.

If I don't look at you
then you cannot see me.

I stare at the curtains,
into the dwindling fire,
at the floor,
shifting my eyes around the shrinking walls.

How long do you watch me?
Waiting for the sign that you have won
and shamed me into loathing what I am.

You sigh and look up at the ceiling,
blow out a huge breath
and then beckon me over
and I crawl,
smaller
than I've ever felt.

I creep over to you,
whispering apologies
until you gather me up
and rock me on your lap.


## NO RETURN

Have we always been so far apart?

Once I would have said anything to please you –
bought any book
for my shelf.
I frittered away my student loans on poetry,
licked words and lines,
ate up the images, plates full of rhymes,
in case it helped to
bring you closer. I'd reel you in with
signifiers, I thought –
searching shelves high and low for
a shibboleth
that meant we understood
one another.

I carried around copies of
Donne
Byron
Yeats

but it was Shakespeare
that made
you stop

one afternoon and ask me what
I thought
of sonnet fifty-seven.

It was a test.

I thought fast,
weighing the book in my hands,
trying to feel my way into its pages,
wondering if I'd even read that one
or if I'd understood anything, ever.
I had to say something,
you were waiting,
hot stutter of embarrassment
and the choke of stupidity
tight at my throat,
I couldn't tell you
I hadn't read it
yet,
so I guessed –
improvised
that it was written for
Will's young man,
and I said that it spoke to me
of passion
unfulfilled.

'I reckon he's just,
you know, like,
really longing for what
he can't have,
for what's beyond his reach –
but it's beautiful, you know,
and unique.
He just wants to be with him.'

You nodded, sun in your eyes, and said,
'Indeed.'
Swallowed your laugh,
then stepped into the shade
and leaned closer,
whispered,

almost touching me,
'"Being your slave, what should I do but tend
Upon the hours and times of your desire?"'
A pause, then a wink,
I think.
'Couldn't put it better, myself,
right, Emma?'

You raised an eyebrow.
Stepped back.
I died
right there and then
in the cloisters,
on the stone,
clutching the book to my chest
and fixing words,
staining myself with the thought that
something had just happened.

Calling up my dad for money later
he asked me how I was and I told him,
'Good. Brilliant, actually.
But, I'm skint, Dad,
can you send me two hundred quid?'

He never said no
and never asked
where all his money was going.

As an investment it turns out
you've been pretty
shit.

# HILARY TERM

## ONWARDS

New starts are as clichéd as
resolutions
already unmade
and I promise myself nothing
one Monday morning,
January fierce with frost
as I make my way across the quad
over the path,
keeping off the iced grass,
inside, and out of the cold,
to where she's waiting.

Margaret Browning.
*No relation*, she said,
the day we first met.

I think she recognized something in me,
the same girl-from-suburbia
anxiety.
I liked her style,
the scarves, tumbled black hair,
the I-don't-give-a-shit-how-I-look stare.
She wore shoes handmade in Italy
and bright colours – orange,
green – didn't care how she clashed
or how much of the room she took up.
Tall and loud, she noticed me
in my first year and told me I was
*Good.*

It was considered, thoughtful;
head on one side

she said:
*You could get a first if you try*,
handing back the essay I'd spent hours
on in the library,
at my desk,
desperate to produce something she might admire.

At the time
I supposed she said that to everyone,
surmised she didn't really have that much faith in me
after all, *could* was only hinting at possibility.
But I left her room
flushed with hope,
ambition, wanting to be
just like her.

I read her remarks,
a scribbled page of notes,
over and over and over again.

Today she greets me
with a smile,
but I feel its hesitation
a reticence I've earned:
she knows my reputation
knows about Tom, supposes that it began
when I was an undergrad, that somewhere along the line
I wasn't entirely honest
or straight with her.
Maybe I bluffed my way to my first,
to that poetry prize,
and now the post-grad place
is perhaps also undeserved –

she said as much after finals.
I was celebrating on the lawn,
had drunk too much, smoked something
that wasn't just tobacco and,

high, I laughed when
she asked,
'You know, is it my imagination or is there
something going on?'

I knew what that meant.
Shook my head.
Hugged her, said,
'Thank you for everything, Margaret,
I think I did it, I think it went well.
I hope I've done you proud.'

Scholar's gown flapping round me like a mad bat,
I offered her a glass but she declined,
disappeared out of the quad taking her
approval with her.

'How can I help? It's been a little while,'
she says now, gesturing that I should sit down.
'I'm pleased to see you –
you look well.
Although you never did get back to me
about that talk.
Or answer my emails.
I was starting to wonder . . .'

I'm surprised she noticed.
I thought she'd soon forget,
and I thought I looked like shit today,
although I suppose I tried
this morning
to paint on a face,
zipped myself into a skirt and
buttoned up a shirt,
pulled on a warm coat,
hooked in earrings,
made myself up:
serious mature student look.

No lipstick,
neat hair,
the merest touch of blusher.

I stare at the faded rug,
the reds and pinks like fire under my feet,
and the bookcases
dark with mystery.

I still want to be her
but I am no closer
and I want to reach out and touch her skin
that is soft and brown,
her hands full of gold rings that glitter,
caught by the glint of lamps;
the magic of the place
brews here.

'Margaret,' I cough, find the words,
'I want to get back on track,
I know it's been a while
but I'm really thinking now
that, perhaps,
if you'd supervise me
I'd get it done –
my doctorate –
earn my DPhil.
I'm determined. Honestly.
I know I can.'

Sceptical, she struggles to keep the
disbelief from tugging at her lips,
instead, nods slowly,
and wonders why
I've changed my mind.
Isn't Tom my supervisor,
is there a problem?
She didn't realize.

(Wonderful news, by the way, she adds,
to hear of his new book –
such exciting times.)

'It's been a tough few months,' I say.
'But a fresh start, I think,
will help.
And you know what I'm like,
you know I'll work really hard.
To be honest it's just the last section,
the period before the end of Mew's life,
where I've hit a block.'

Confidence is something I've learned to fake
and now put on –
it is the face I will unpeel
as soon as I'm out of here,
when I will stand
flat against a cold stone wall
and wrap my fingers around my hair
and pull it from my scalp,
instead of screaming and
letting Margaret see how close I am
to vanishing,
how little of me is left.

'If Tom agrees,
I don't see why not.
I'm interested, I must admit.'

I want to kiss her,
sit here, in this room,
for the rest of my days
while she watches me work
like a little girl
at a schoolroom desk,
observed and nurtured,
praised into being the best she can be.

I've missed that,
need a mentor, a friend.
Don't want to tell Margaret I love her –
instead I say,
*Thank you.*
*Thank you.*
'I'll send you what I've done.
I promise I won't let you down.'

Second chance granted,
I gallop down the stairs
across the quad, fly up into town.


## APPETITE

Ari would taste like
a picnic by the river:
cold roast chicken,
white wine
and sunshine.

He has gold hair, cheekbones,
summer looks and a summer smile,
and is not my type
on paper.

Not as tall as you, Tom, nor as strong,
but he has nice eyes and
his long hair today is twisted half up
into a top-knot.
There's a bit of a swagger to his stride,
a nonchalant slouch
as if he knows he's cool,
and I'm not and I like
watching him.

The lack of complexity turns me on
and I'm thinking about what it would be like to kiss him
instead of you
when I should be listening to the things
he's saying about my poems.

He holds the book like it might break,
as if it's porcelain –

'God, I love your stuff,
it's so stark, you know,
but so full of hope –
and
raw – like you've pulled out your insides
and offered them up.
You're talented, Emma,
amazing, really.'

He sounds surprised.
I try to smile but the compliments are flat,
flaccid, wet sponge,
they flop, don't stick.

I don't want to talk about this now.

I want to tell him about Margaret.
I want him to know what I'm planning,
want to tell him everything that you, Tom, said to me,
how you humiliated me
and that I'm going to start again
and do everything better
without you.

I need to announce
that I don't need you.

But the steam from hot tea
fills my face so I can't see Ariel's eyes,

can't read him properly
although he's opposite me
and I think about his knees only centimetres from mine,
wonder if he cares that I'm twenty-six.
It's only a couple of years between us,
hardly a lifetime,
I am hardly old –
although there will be women, girls
he likes better,
with whom he'd rather spend his time.
Fun people,
funny people,
clever and astute.
He won't want to hear me whine.
And it's clear how he feels about you.
If it were a choice between us
I know who'd win.


I say *thank you* when he pauses
and take back my book,
lift it out of his hands.
There is the remnant of a tan,
sun-bleached hair at his wrists,
and I suspect he skis.
His hands are capable,
gentle, soft and firm;
I imagine them near my neck,
his breath in my hair,
the heat of a body that wants me.
I want to leave my palm in his, take
whatever it is he's offering,


but I slip my book back into my bag
and cough, look away and smile.


'So, what are you writing now?'

'Nothing,' I say, which is stupid because
he'll want to know why,
and that will destroy
the picture of me that was starting to form.

I want him to see me
garret bound,
bashing out poems
on a typewriter, living the life of a poet
on the Left Bank in Paris.
I want him to fantasize
about my sonnets,
want him to prize
my use of synecdoche
above all other uses of
synecdoche
and all the time I will
be taking him apart
stripping him down to his constituent parts.

I will put each one in my mouth,
test it, try it out,
nibble, suck, taste,
swallow
what I like.

I sip my tea.
He lifts the pot
offers me another cup and
I think I like him more and more.

                    ∽


'Where to now?'
It's almost four
and Ariel tells me he has a lecture,
it's a late one, with *the prof*,
and I shrug, button up my coat,

wrap my scarf around my neck and turn to go
as Ari takes my hand and says,
'You should come with,
when did you last see him strut his stuff?'

Oh, if only he knew
how I have internalized
every phrase, every sign – how I know
the way you will run your hand
over your head,
turning to show your best side,
and how every joke is timed
to elicit maximum laughter.
I know how you will decide
which students you will invite
into your confidence,
whose work you will read
with extra care
and whose you will hand back
with barely a mark to show your attention rested there.

It is a kind of warfare.

When you handed back my essays
marked up with your immaculate hand
or even despoiled:
lines scoring through paragraphs
and your marginalia
telling me what I'd written was
*Guff* –
that sharpened HB pencil always poised
to mete out critique,
an occasional *Yes, indeed!*
I took every word as evidence
of my relevance,
or not.

In my first term
you'd invited us all
to come to a particular lecture –
an evening event –
and I felt special,
couldn't wait to hear what you had to say
or to feel my brain expanding
under the pressure of yours.

Was it then you talked about Victorian radicals
and the poverty of invention?
Art's state of winter, and
the reinvigorating power of ancient minds?

I took notes,
pages of wild, excited points –
the details I don't remember,
but what I see
is that room: gracious, ancient, and you, Tom,
up there at the front
catching my eye, nodding,
making certain to show you noticed me,
front row.

Tonight we sneak in at the back.
It's a full house,
you can still pull in a crowd.

The girls will want you to look at them
the way I wanted you to look at me,
boys too, Ariel is nervy
with anticipation.
They need to feel you approve,
perhaps they fantasize about you
taking off their clothes.
It's so boring how
they want to be the Sylvia to your Ted
and imagine you taking them to bed.

'What's he talking about?' I ask.
Ari settles in beside me.
'Fin de siècle.
Bound to be top-notch.
And useful for you too, right?'

Consigned to a minor role
in literature's roll call of the greats
I've been fascinated with my poet
ever since I stumbled across her at seventeen
lurking in some dusty anthology.
Poor Charlotte,
who was brilliant, but who nobody reads.

I told you, one morning, lying in bed,
that I wanted to resurrect her,
one day write a book –
make her important:
did you think I could?

You laughed and said,
'One step at a time,
But hey, why not? Let's see.'
And after that you supervised,
read my chapters as I typed up,
until suddenly I stopped –

stuck –

couldn't see where this was going
and told you that I
needed time.

That was when it started to go bad.
Or maybe after you blamed me for the fact that you
were such a useless father –
the day your daughter wouldn't come with you
when you arrived to pick her up

and cried and howled
legs thrashing against your thighs
when you lifted her into your arms,
still wailing that she hated you.

I stood several steps behind you
on the street
and you looked at me
your mouth twisting your face into ugliness.

However, I wait to hear what it is you
have for us today.
Maybe you can shed light
on my current predicament,
my anxiety
about where this century will take me,
because it feels as if we are roaring towards
disaster, always on the verge
of some terrible collapse,
skirting it only by sheer luck,
not judgement.

(Judgement is something no one seems to have.)

I shrink in the seat,
wind my scarf higher,
but Ariel pulls off his jacket,
settles in with his laptop,
long fingers fast on the keys.

I fold my arms,
unwrap a sweet,
sit silently sucking,
I close my eyes
and wonder how visibly invisible
I am

because I still want you to know
I'm here,

want you to acknowledge me,
to notice me
even if you hate me –
and later when we get home,
tell me you're sorry
and we will
begin again
falling in love
and do it better this time.

Here you are.
Handsome.
Smart.

(I ironed that shirt.)

I can't help it, I sit up.

You pause on your way to the front –
say something I can't hear
and I lean forward
want to see who it is
you're speaking to,
which girl on the front row
has caught your attention,
stopped you in your tracks.

Heads turn.
It isn't only me who wants to know
what I've missed.
I'm jealous of whatever it is.

I have loved your voice,
known its every tone
in the quiet of love
and the cold of despair

and now it's distant –

there is a space between
what you say,
what you think
and what I know.

The room stills,
settling into expectation.

You begin
with a joke,
always with a joke
(get them on side
make them smile),
and then –

at first I don't recognize it –

don't quite realize –

just feel an uncanny sense
of having been here before,
that I'm looking in a mirror,
seeing my other side
in some other life,
the fantasy I've forgotten.

But the blare of an alarm
makes me open my eyes
as it begins to make sense –

there are
words
flying
up into your mouth
from a typewritten page –

Chapter Two –

in which I wrote about
the threat of madness, the wrack of time
and the buried heart
that lurked within the poetess's rage

(they always call her poetess,
                    the old white men who hold the keys
and I wanted to wrest them      out of those twisted fingers
              rattle and snatch and drag us forward,

  leave them staring,      jowls flapping,      fingers grasping

              and if the key wouldn't turn then we'd
stand screaming                          through
              the gaps,
                  I'd bend the metal with my bare hands
                      and twist it into new shapes,
                          break out of all bounds
                              to create
                                  something
                                      new).

I tune in again
shift the thud from my ears and
press my heart back down into my chest
squeeze it tight through the narrow ridges of my throat
choking
on
the
lump of it
solid mass
of
disgust
for you
and myself.

Foghorns blare.

You speak into the cacophony
and make them laugh again
with *my* jokes, which are actually good,
on which I spent hours,
trying not to let myself lose
the thread, never fumbling the needle,
stitching something
magnificent out of my material,
and you deliver a close reading
that I slaved over,
the thrill of the adrenalin that day,
Bodleian bound,
as her world came alive in my mind,
panting over the poems as they danced,
my brain flashing
with insight, the sudden understanding
of what my poet meant:
that she didn't care
if you wouldn't feel
what she felt,
that it wasn't the point;
that there was always so much more to it than that.

You take it all,
give it to them,
tease out the complexities of tense,
until they're nearly crying
when you bring out her end, those last days:
that terrible death.

You lay my Charlotte out on the slab,
rinsed clean with swallowed disinfectant,
holes burnt into her heart
fearing life
going mad.

As you deliver
what I created –

spent hours over, germinated, propagated –
I watch what little there was of us left,
see it
roll away
like a penny towards a drain.

As you narrate my words –
stolen,
lifted out of my mouth
and translated into yours –

as I hear myself on your lips
and you pass off
my thesis
as your own work

I understand.

*Fucking cunt*, I whisper under my breath,
stand up,
push past the other students
not caring
who I offend
who I trample on
nudge or shove.

Bursting out into the vestibule,
I run past the library,
down the steps
and out into the hard white air.

⮾

I realize I have measured out my life
in lies,
lost myself
whilst I spent so long asking
who I was.

What an appalling waste of time.

If I'd howled, as I should have done
the second you began,
if I'd shouted
*Liar, bastard, scum,*
they'd have escorted me out,
sedated me.
I would have been designated
hysterical.

Put me in that box why don't you, *Prof,*
lock me in the attic,
chain me to a bedpost,
leave me there to rot.

*Plagiarism begins at home –*
I should have been warned.

Can see Fitzgerald's Zelda,
Dorothy Wordsworth,
Véra Nabokov
shaking their heads and
shrugging their shoulders.
Hasn't history taught me anything?

I have spent the last year concussed
but now my brain is waking up,
firing electric shocks
as I make connections, begin to understand
what you are and what you've done.

❧

At home, dripping,
gasping, sweating, out of breath,
I grab my laptop,
fumbling fingers,

tapping foot,
coat still on.

I need to see it,
find the pages
and those precious hours
spent glued to my spot
breathing in books,
waiting for treasure to be unearthed from the stacks.

I need the evidence of your theft.
Evidence I'm not going mad.
When was it you sat here
in this room,
on my chair,
plundering my work
that you'd told me wasn't quite yet
there?

*Remember, Emma, you'll have to defend this*
*to a panel of scholars*
*and they won't go easy*
*just because you've been published once.*

You like to remind me
I'm a one-hit wonder
and I have internalized that fact,
bought into your version of me
as insufficient, inadequate: a fraud.

*You haven't lived up to your potential,*
*and you're not ready yet.*

I search the files.
Disorderly, disorganized,
like my mind that moves too fast leaving
the rest of me behind.
But it shouldn't be hard to locate

that part:
the bit you took
and passed around
the lecture hall today
as if it were a tray of appetizers,
invited them to gobble it up
then later belch out their praise,
crediting you with the original thought.

I want to snatch it back.
Ram my fingers down throats
reclaim my words.
I wish I'd never shown you,
trusted you,
believed you,
when you said it wasn't good enough –
*I* wasn't good enough –
yet.

My fingers rattle over the keys
as I type in search terms:
Charlotte
Mew
Chapter
Two

But nothing –
empty pages
blank
no words here now,
what was
has been
erased,      deleted,      stolen.

It's                              gone.

If she's not here –
my poet –

then maybe I too am thin air,
maybe I've been vanishing

because if
you haven't seen me
and I haven't heard my own voice
then I am just a stump;
a bloody, amputated tongue.

No.
If the file is gone
I will find the paper
I wrote those words upon –

I have notes,
piles of scrawl,
and the printed version
I was going to nitpick through.
The labour of months
that was becoming too many years
until I stopped:
doubting my direction,
uncertain that any of it was any good.

⌒

You liked telling me it would be all right.
Last summer
we chatted over coffee, standing in the garden
you admired my beds
said I was making our life pretty
and you told me it was normal,
writer's block;
not to worry that I was running out of money,
needed to take on a job
to pay my fees, for food,
my share of the bills, my debts.
You liked having me around and

maybe I could
wait tables, or type up another writer's notes?

I failed to shout that I was neither muse
nor amanuensis,
I was more than that,
could do better,
searched for a way to make it clear
that I didn't want to stop,

I wanted to know how to go on.

'Why don't I take on some teaching?' I said
but you thought that was perhaps asking too much,
might prove more of a hindrance than a help
and distract me when I should be focusing
on finding a way through to the end.
I nodded, agreed, slowly said yes,
I wasn't ready to get into that yet –

I'll admit the thought of it frightened me,
maybe I was relieved when you advised against.

You told me to take my time,
not to stress, to let it rest.
Sometimes it's a bit like bread –
you have to leave the dough alone,
let it rise,
and then open the drawer
and find it there,
a surprise of ideas – fresh and swollen
like flesh.

I smiled at the analogy and agreed,
surprised you when I
began to knead
my own loaves;
you laughed and pulled me on to your knee

and kissed me,
dusted with flour that fell from my hands
(cheap domestic confetti
that stuck in my hair, flecked our clothes;
and startled, later, undressing, I thought it was
my skin flaking,
that I was breaking down
into pieces,
anatomized – expecting a little finger, a nostril,
a heel or
my heart
to fall out of my bra).

⮑

I turn the house upside down
and inside out,
every corner, nook and cranny,
search for what I've lost,
the evidence that I am not making this up.

Sneezing in the dust,
on my hands and knees I scour
and scrabble
think about pulling up floorboards,
prising wood with my bare hands
and bleeding into the bones of the house
until I find it.
Her.
My work.
Charlotte somewhere,
somehow gone.

## DUEL

The key turns in the front door
and I rush from the kitchen
and stand in the hall, ready.

You laugh at me
when you turn to take me in.

I don't see what's funny
what's provoked your derision –
am I a sideshow now
as well as everything else?

'What's wrong?'
Your face falls when you realize
I'm not smiling,
when you understand this isn't a game,
that the way I'm looking at you and holding my knife
is real.

No more creeping or crawling,
no smoothing things over,
impersonating contrition in the hope of love.

I have to confront this.

You hold out a bunch of flowers
and
a question mark hangs suspended,
threaded with pollen,
an orange stain of warning not to trust this gesture.

'Emma?'

Did you see me in your lecture?
I don't think you know what I heard.

Did you see me leaving?
I don't think you have a clue what I know.

You stare at the knife,
frowning, perhaps
beginning to see.

Do you understand
that maybe I could put it against your throat?

You say my name again, take a step closer
as I step away,
still offering the stinking lilies,
and I smash them to the floor.

'Em? What's wrong?'

I don't have the words
to explain
*what is*
*wrong*
when the answer is,
*Everything.*

'How dare you?'
I begin, already weak.
You dare because – why wouldn't you?
You're used to helping yourself
to other people's things,
to helping yourself to me.
No one has ever said no to you
and so your fair share
has never been enough.

And here we are
with our flowers and knives,
playing out the same old scenes.

I try again.
I have to say it.
Why can't I say it?

'You're despicable, Tom.'
I wave my weapon
in the direction of your dick
and know that I've gone wrong already
that now I just look ridiculous,
small and pale and ugly.
A mouse gnawing on a corner of life.

I should be throwing things,
hurling pots and pans.
Wish you were tied up
and I was aiming arrows,
sharp-eyed, dart fast,
pinning you like a specimen
carefully spreadeagled against the
fading Farrow & Ball –
targeting your weakness,
aiming for your heart.

But – no – wrong again,
it's fortified,
fully armoured,
and nothing I can say will
make you feel a fraction of the pain
I feel.
The pain you deserve.

'Emma, put down the knife –
are you buttering toast? Did something break?
Tell me what's happened,
I can see you're distressed –
what is it?
Your time of the month?'

It's my turn to laugh.
Here we go.
It always comes back to that –
my womb, how I bleed too much, make a mess
of the sheets each month.

Well: fuck you.

'I know what you've done,' I say.
'And?
What do you mean?'
You wait,
calm, hands held up
as if you can charm me, snake-eyed,
into submission.
But I have turned
rancid and will not be soothed.

'And?'
I spit my incredulity into your face
but you don't react.
Who will break first?
Who will say what needs to be said?

'I went to your lecture.'

You take off your coat,
put down your bag,
begin to walk past me
through the hallway to the kitchen.
You don't touch me as you
open the fridge and take out a bottle,
pour a glass,
steady hand,
and I laugh when
you don't offer me
anything –

just watch me watching you – and then you shrug
and walk past me again,
throwing words over your shoulder:

'Did you learn anything, then?'

I scream, follow you,
snarling in rage.
'What? You're not my tutor any more –
or my supervisor,
mentor,
any of that shit!
You can shove it, Tom.
You're a liar
and a cheat.
You're basically just a pathetic thief.'

My words hit the wall of your back,
crumbling as I stamp and say,
'This is it –
exactly –
you are the inventor
of ways to make me feel
small.'

I will smash my way free
from where I am penned,
dismantle the walls
emerge out of this cell –

I swear at you again,
call you every name I can think of,
yell and accuse,
'You're a fraud
everyone knows it, Tom,
everyone sees
you just can't cut it any more,
it's pathetic. Truly. You're an absolute joke.'

## SCHOOLED

Something hits.
You tense, body tightening,
tuning in to the key of rage.

'I'm what?'

'You heard.'
I take a step back.
'You're a laughing stock.'

You turn, whip fast,
sweep an arm along the shelf,
grab a book
and slam it down between us.
You grab another, fling it on to your pile
and begin to build a tower.

'I see. Well. Here's my work, Emma,
now, please, why don't you share yours?'

You grab my arm,
slam the door before I can leave,
catch me, and draw me close.

'Oh no, you don't get to walk away.
It doesn't work like that. Not if you want to start
throwing accusations around.
Now, let's see. What have we here?'

You hold me
in hands that I hadn't believed would hurt me
but now I think might
as you pick my notebook out of my bag.

I twist, squirm, push back
with my heels on your shins,

my nails on your skin,
wrestling in a python's grip, constricted,
my brain simmering as your muscles tense.

You flick to a page of my illegible scrawl.
'Read it to me, Emma, please.'

I won't.
*No, get off.*

Immobilized, you direct my head
towards my words.
'I'm waiting, Emma. Now. Come on.'

And I have to do it.
To read the poem that isn't a poem but
an abortive thing, trivial
and stinking in its weak metaphor
as I compare myself to
breeding maggots,
soft larvae that live on rotten meat.

No one speaks.

It hangs there
between us.
A butchered sonnet.

'Interesting, I'm sure.
Shall we talk you through where this
goes wrong?
The problem with the tenor
and the vehicle?
The volta that isn't a volta?
The weak execution of form?'

I shake my head.
You lick a finger, flick to another page and we perform

the same routine. I want to run
but can't move, just
butt my head back against your chest.
'Tom,          stop it,          please.'
You sigh and softly pose your next question
as you begin to loosen
your grip:
'Now then, Emma. Who wrote this?'

The first book from your pile is in my face
forced up before my eyes
under my nose
so close to my mouth
I begin to choke.

'Come on, Emma, don't be a baby, tell me,
what does it say?'

Your fingers dig up my skin
as if it is soil,
planting the only answer there is.
Choking, I stutter out your name.

You take another book, repeat the act,
working methodically through the stack,
and I wait for something better to come out of my
      mouth –
bats, or beetles, a swarm of wasps –
instead it is just the admission
of your brilliance.

We're done.
You check your watch, step back, stretch.
'Wonderful. Now we're getting somewhere,
Alpha bloody plus.
It seems we have the message clear now, yes?'

You look at me, touch my cheek,
'Although you'll have to see someone.
This behaviour isn't normal. You do realize that?'

Book held like a
missile you could launch at my head,
you wait for me to acquiesce before you wave me away,

bored of this game.


## RAW

Beaten, I back out
of the room
sink to the floor
crawl up the stairs
curl up
in the dark spare room
and breathe into the carpet
dreaming of screaming at yellow walls.

What did I do?
You have never hurt me
like that
before.

Was it deserved?
Just punishment for my insolence?
For failing, not being good enough –
for taking something
that was never mine –
a prize that should have gone to
someone serious
who knew
more about masculine rhyme
or the bloody sublime.

It's karma,
fate
or maybe God striking me
for having too much pride.
Hubris – everyone's favourite
fatal flaw.

And you, Tom.
You
are the master
of it all.


## ESCAPE

I try not to cry.
Tell myself that there is no point to this pain
unless I can use it.
But my eyes leak and my nose runs
and I cannot make myself small enough.

I jump at the knock on the door
and cough out words
that you interpret as permission to bring me
breakfast in bed.

You deliver it to the spare room
where I barely slept
and sit beside me, perched on an edge,
gazing at the bookshelves
as I sip tea
and stare at toast going cold, a scraping of jam,
pathetic portion of muesli
floating in milk.

You look at me,
stroke my hair, dab at my tears and say,

'Emma, what's wrong?
I'm worried,
last night – you didn't come to bed,
you weren't yourself –
are you feeling better yet?'

Are we pretending it never happened?
Is it going to be one of those things we never mention again?

Like
the time in Greece –
another holiday you paid for –
we stayed in a tiny hotel
by the water,
I lay in the sun every day
and at night
I melted in the heat,
oozed like butter
all over the sheets.

(That was the part you enjoyed but
you said we could have stayed at home
and done it for free.)

During the day you tried to sleep
disturbed by the noise of the cicadas
and stood beneath an olive tree
as if you might find the culprit
rasping above you.

Some friends you knew from school
or your undergraduate days
were passing on their boat –
we met them in a bay,
swaying over duckboards towards a restaurant
perched at the water's edge.
You were twitchy, already tense;
the restaurant was

classy, expensive,
and I wasn't sure
I liked the sense
that everyone there
knew something
I didn't.

They were wearing white,
blond and tanned,
blue-eyed,
and I itched the sunburn on my neck,
a pale imitation of them.
You matched those blue-eyed smiles with yours,
fell right back into a different kind of self.
But these were the type of people that made me clam up
or do something
utterly
inappropriate.

We ate every kind of fish
and oysters,
scallops, prawns,
and drank bottles and bottles
of cold, dry white.

Before I went to university
I didn't know that people were eating supper
when I had tea,
or lunch
when I had dinner,
that Marmite could become a delicacy
in the hands of a Wykehamist
making me toast.
I didn't recognize the voice
that came out of my mouth
that night.
I started elongating my vowels
but I swore a lot – said *fuck* too much

and laughed at them
when they looked
a little aghast.

So what, I thought, I'm *coarse*,
your bit of rough.
If that's my part
I might as well play it well.

You used to like your poet
with a navvy's tongue,
used to think it was
authentic –
it turned you on that I came on strong,

so I stopped bullshitting,
stopped trying to smooth my way into their confidence –
started to laugh at their expense:
*Snobs*, I said.
*Bunch of twats.*
I'd heard them sneering at another girl's taste,
mocking that she'd never read
anything more taxing
than chick lit, for heaven's sake.

Your hand moved on to my arm,
then on to my back and
I wondered if you'd cover my mouth,
could almost feel myself
sinking my teeth
into flesh,
gnawing your wrist,
iron and salt at the back of my throat,
my stomach beginning to heave.
So when they invited us back to the boat
you said: *No,*
*thank you* –
we had to go.

Perhaps there was some sign
you gave that I missed
because they
*Completely understood, darling,*
and kissed you goodbye
on both cheeks.

I heard them laughing
as they took to the moonlit beach,
shoes off,
paddling, pushing each other
squealing into the sea,
a tumble of blond heads
white jeans
silk shirts
gold rings.

What was so sophisticated about that?
Why wasn't I
part of that set?
I could paddle too,
take off my clothes
and swim naked in the warm, dark water.

You shook your head,
took my hand,
and said, 'Let's go,'
and took me back to bed.

Now when you see those people –
if you see those people –
you don't tell me.
I'm disinvited,
I am
decidedly
infra dig
(a phrase I learned
from Enid Blyton,

which proves Latin
isn't just for privileged pricks).

Maybe they thought I was rough
or just that I was an idiot.
I don't care
any more.

I bite my toast,
spray crumbs
and wonder if you've laced it
with a drug,
if I am to be narcotized
into silence today.

Would I prefer it if you fucked me quiet
like you used to?
Maybe then at least I wouldn't feel
like I'm dying.

I cough, splutter,
tea spilling
on to the covers,
and you tell me to *Shhh*
as you mop up the mess.
*Not to worry,*
*it's just tea,*
you'll wash the sheets
while I get dressed.

I don't know why you're being so nice
and I don't buy this act –
but I'll improvise.

We step around each other,
you skirt my wounds,
try to cheer me up with compliments –
or maybe you're just trying
to make me forget.

I lock the bathroom door,
breathe in
resolution
and cast about for someone to help me.

Maryanne will have a plan.
She is a woman who knows
how to throw shit right back
at whoever hurled it.

My mum used to say we were
attached at the hip
and now I wish
she were nearer,
closer,
that she hadn't moved
halfway across the world,
whole time zones between us.

You bash about
downstairs
and I pack for that trip,
throwing things in my bag,
plotting a ticket bought with your card:
one-way.
I fantasize about Columbia, Harvard, Yale –
a fresh start.

You bellow,
'Emma? All right?'
I jump, shout back,
'Yes, I'm fine.'

You begin to sing –
opera today –
and I close the door to block out the noise.

You are happy.
And I am about to scuttle away from the mess you've
made of my life.
Do I let you get away with it?
I imagine Maryanne, Margaret Browning,
Charlotte Mew,
think about what they'd do.

Charlotte would never take this shit from you.

I try to order my thoughts,
make sense out of your senselessness.
Maybe I won't abscond.
Perhaps I'll stay close,
following you,
waiting for the chance
to serve myself this time –
because I have to fight back,
don't I?

Why should you have this?
Why should I run?

Because I'm clever too,
let's not forget,
clever enough to set a trap
to catch you out.
I know how you work,
have spent years observing
how the gears shift
into reverse
when you're cornered
only to let you speed away fast,
but I can turn
and turn again
on you
and them.

## MANOEUVRES

Think.

Your bag.
Last night,
when you came home,
where did you put it?
Usual spot?

I creep downstairs –
I know which steps creak
and spread my weight carefully.
On tiptoe,
I sneak
behind your back.
The radio's on
and you're listening to Strauss,
humming, conducting
as you make coffee,
fry eggs,
still in your dressing gown,
no idea that I'm up.
Joyous violins soar
and I almost dance
to the soundtrack of deception –
a trickster's score –
flitting like a bat
swiftly into your study.

There it is.
I rummage
inside the folds and pockets,
turning over your things,
flicking through papers
with quick, careful fingers.
The memory stick
slips into my palm

like a coin
passed in hope of good luck.
I pocket it and sneak back upstairs.

Sweating and hot, and then flashes of cold,
I wait for you to leave the house.

Civil, we smile at one another
and the sun washes us
with a little bleak light
as we undertake little tasks:
you help unstack the dishwasher
unasked
and even put some washing on.
I thank you,
help you to find
the right setting and
my smile grows
leaden as
I perform appropriate gratitude for
all the little kindnesses:
cups of coffee,
a biscuit,
a kiss on the top of my head.

I know you're watching me.
I watch you back
and pretend.
I clean up the dead flowers that litter the hall,
and pick up the books from the living-room floor
and replace them carefully on the shelves.
I creak from chore to chore.

You haven't showered,
shaved,
you don't care that you stink.
I wonder if you're going to work.

'I thought perhaps
I'd stay at home.
Make sure all's well.'

'Why wouldn't it be?
Yesterday, I was just a bit pissed.
I'm fine, you know how I can get.'

You kiss my cheek as you pass,
squeeze my shoulder and when I flinch
you offer sympathy,
ask if I'm sore, have been hurt,
as if I am an invalid.
(Indeed I have been invalidated –
but that's a different matter.)

My neck aches
and my bruises are swelling –
you offer arnica cream
and are gentle, tender.

Your fingers knead my shoulder.
Perhaps I am the dough,
the loaf
you will bake –
will you
put me in the oven
and later butter my brain?

While we've busied ourselves
this morning
I have been questioning, thinking,
trying to understand.
Why didn't you just write your own bloody book?

I'd like to mock you with that thought,
jeer at the man
who won't read novels

written by women –
at least not if they're still alive –
point out the irony of your current situation

but I don't.

I keep it clean, mundane,
as if my thoughts only dwell on household things,
the timetable of domestic undertakings.
'Don't forget you need to pick up
the girls tonight,' I say,
glancing at the calendar,
remembering
that it is your day
to play daddy,
doing the thinking for you.

You nod as if you hadn't forgotten,
although I read the signs
elsewhere –
the sudden spill of coffee on the arm of the chair
tells me that you hadn't made
the connection,
didn't remember that it's Tuesday.

You scratch your fingers through your beard,
look at me, imploringly –
'I've got to go out after all.
Will you get something for their supper?
You're so good at that,
you know what children like
better than me.'

I refuse to infer
that I'm being infantilized
although the look in your eyes
confirms

your disdain –
a flash of that scorn:
I'm an adequate maid.


I think of all the times
I have crouched on the carpet with your girls,
played with their dolls
or read them stories.
I think of all the times
at the park,
pushing them on swings
when you've had to work;
waiting in the quad
with a toddler and a baby
who weren't mine.
But I didn't mind.
I love your daughters
maybe more than you do,
and your ex, Hannah,
is all right –
I think she and I
might find we have
more in common than I realized.


'Yes, OK,' I say,
'but I don't feel up to the walk.
Can you let Hannah know
that she'll have to drop them off?'


You frown – put out; you hate to text
or call your ex-wife,
as if it's a sign of weakness
to change a plan,
negotiate a compromise
with a woman you loathe.
'Can't you take the bus?' you sigh.

'All right.' I let you deflect
my tiny demand,
let you believe that you
command my time
as always,
but this inflexibility, this willingness to send me
and your kids
on an hour's round journey
in the rain,
tells me that you really
don't give a shit how I am.

But.
I have your memory stick
safe in my hand.


## MARY FUCKING POPPINS

I've got a brolly
and my bag
crackling with tiny plastic packages
full of the sweets
you disapprove of,
bought deliberately
to piss you off.
I feel a little bit like
a fairy-tale witch
building a gingerbread house
to tempt your daughters with.

But a little bit of sugar
never hurt
and the girls
like treats –
don't we all?
And although you won't know

they'll have filled their faces –
giggled, sugar high,
on the bus home –
I will
and that will be enough to make me
smile.


Hannah opens the door to her house,
pretty North Oxford Regency villa –
once you divorced, she married a banker
and she writes too.
But Hannah's screenplay
has been optioned for TV:
a Netflix original,
sure-fire hit.
You sneered when you heard
as if her success was trivial, unearned,
and I wish I'd said then
that you were being mean.


I ask her how she is,
wish she'd ask me in for coffee,
and let me tell her everything.


But she's rushing,
looks harassed,
gathers up the girls and their bags,
reminds me they have homework to do.
Martha – just five –
and seven-year-old Tabitha
who has your way
of looking at me
with narrowed eyes,
suspicious of my intentions.
Hannah hands me their things
and apologizes for loading me down
with all the paraphernalia of parenthood.

'Thanks, Emma,
I suppose Tom couldn't make the time?'

I almost deny,
almost defend you,
but instead I say,
'Yup, that's right,
Tom's a busy man, Hannah.'

She rolls her eyes.
'I've had his mother on the phone,
she wants to see the girls.
But I'm not taking them
all that way –
he'll have to sort it out with her.
It's not my responsibility any more.'

'Who'd want to go anyway?' I banter back.
'It's a house of bloody misery.
And Annette's a bitch.'

Hannah snorts a laugh,
swishes her long blonde hair
and we smile,
share a moment
of complicity.

She was never the enemy.

You never told me you had kids
when we started this thing;
it might have been worth mentioning.

The girls and I sing songs:
'The Wheels on the Bus',
'The Grand Old Duke of York',
and tell stories
in which the princess comes out on top.

Then Tabitha wants to know
as I open the front door
when her daddy will be home.

'Interesting question,' I say.
'Call him
and ask.'
I put my phone on speaker
pass it into her hands.

You answer impatiently,
thinking it's me,
apparently there is no further need to be polite,
and Tabbie's face pales,
shocked,
not used to being spoken to
like that.

'When are you here, Daddy?'
she demands
and I admire her tone –
she won't take any shit
from you
or any bloke.

You tell her: 'Soon,'
and mutter other
placatory words
as I set up paints and paper
on the kitchen table,
turn on the oven to cook
your daughters' tea
and pour myself a large drink.

Tabitha insists the homework gets done,
so I wipe up ketchup and spilt juice
and we begin.

Her penmanship is outstanding for one so small,
and she crafts a letter
in character as Elizabeth I
ordering her ships to sail,
to set forth, on attack.

We squeeze teabags to age it,
burn the edges with a match,
and I watch the forgery
glowing,
feeling the scratch
of an idea.

You're still not home when it's time for bed
and both of them are crying.
'We want to see Daddy,' Tabitha says,
and I stroke her hair, one daughter on each knee
(I used to babysit all the time,
saving up money for my university dream),
and tell her the lies that you tell me,
'I suppose he's working,
you know he has to work hard.'
(I expect you're actually in the college bar.)
'Don't worry, sweetie,
I'll make sure
he comes straight up
to kiss you goodnight.'

Poor Tabitha is old enough to realize
that she's been sidelined
in favour of
More Important Things.

I sit with her,
give Martha a hug,
wait for them to nod off,
snug, side by side in the spare bed
which I've made up with the covers

that I bought especially for them:
turtles and seahorses,
a laughing whale –

Tabitha traces the outline
of the shark, says
she wants to dive in deep seas
and find lost wrecks.
I think that's a good idea,
better than writing
poems no one reads.
I don't say that, but nod my head
and we make up a tale
about the turtle
who makes friends with a water snake
and they live in a fairground under an ocean
and fly to the moon some nights
when they're fed up.

'Where have you been?' I hiss
when you come in
later than late.
You dump your bag
and coat in the hall
and we face off
as I scold you,
try to make you understand
how your daughters felt.
But you're adamantine;
my words hit the wall
of your indifference
and the excuse I'm so sick of –
'Sometimes work comes first' –
but before you can justify yourself
with a host of lies
I tell you that I'm too tired
to hear it,
too sad for your kids,

and if you refuse to see it
then what can I do?

One of them wakes up crying in the night
and I kick you under the covers,
try to get you to shift, and
you groan,
drag yourself out of bed
as the howls go on,
waking up the other one.

Two wailing daughters.

You stumble off to check they're all right.
It's something, I suppose.
'Just a nightmare,'
you mumble as you groan back into bed.
'Oh, I know,'
I whisper into the sheets
as I listen to your breathing slow,
watch the stars irritate the sky
where the blinds don't meet
and lie awake until dawn.


## HANNAH

Morning chaos of Coco Pops
and unbrushed hair –
the girls already wondering
where their mum is.

It's only half past six
and you've already left.

We don't have a TV
so I put the radio on

and suggest a danceathon.
Martha sucks her thumb
and Tabbie rolls her eyes
far too sophisticated for this sort of caper.

I guess she's her father's daughter.
Instead I read her a story,
plucking Rossetti from the shelf:
terrify them with goblins
if all else fails.

We pore over the pictures –
illustrated scenes of temptation:
whisking tails and seeping fruits,
delicious horrors fill the pages and
I pull out the paper and paints again,
draw outlines for Martha to colour and
she drags the stub of a crayon over a wall.

It's a long two hours
before Hannah arrives.
She's one of the lovely ones,
has one of those faces
stamped with
the certainty of success,
the beauty of symmetry.
I wanted to write my way
into her life.

Yes, I know you screwed her
and then left her when she was pregnant
with your second child,
but she's still one of your lot,
really,
she's nothing like me.

I wonder if you regret
that choice?

Wonder how I tricked you
into thinking I was similarly
blessed, that, for whatever reason,
I could be enough.

Because there's such a thing
as an upper-class face –
it's the face of someone who's rarely had to
make do.

Your sisters,
your mother,
you
and Hannah,
all share that unencumbered brow.

But I've spent too long studying this type
like an anthropologist
trapped with a tribe.
I need to shrug off
the ridiculous chip that greases my shoulder
and renders me
oily with envy and slow
with a burden they don't recognize.

When Hannah knocks on the door
I smile without slyness and hurry to welcome her in;
she never usually hangs about,
whisking her children away as fast as she can.
'Tom's not here.
If you've got a sec
we could have a coffee, a chat.'

She glances at her watch –
is about to make an excuse
but I don't give her a chance,
turn around
walk back to the kitchen:
'I'll stick the kettle on.'

The front door closes and the girls
rush their mum.
As it should be, I think.
I tell her they've been
good as gold
and watch her being
swamped by their love,
cuddled into their arms.
She admires the pictures of goblins
and fairies, unicorns
and castles,
looks at me and says,
'OK, what's up?'

I could cry.
I could beg for help.
I could explain exactly what you've done.

But I'm brought up short
thinking that maybe she won't be on my side,
maybe she'll defend you –
you're the father of these children
and she must have loved you once.

'What's happened?' she continues.
'Let me guess . . .
Another woman?
Are you now
in the position I was?'

When did you first tell me that Hannah existed?
How long was it before I realized
you had a life
that you should have been living?
Maybe I knew and just chose to ignore
the truth of what I was doing.

There were all the reasons
why you couldn't stay
and the early mornings when you lay awake
staring at the ceiling,
checking your watch
then finally leaping up
and disappearing out of the quad,
hurrying somewhere.

You never invited me out
or to your home –
we kissed in your college rooms
or in my student single bed,
the occasional hotel.
I don't deserve Hannah's time.

She knows it, hasn't taken off her coat
or sat down
or picked up the mug
or answered my question –
whether she takes milk –
but she's all I've got
and I sink on to a chair,
put my head in my hands.

'I know you don't owe me,
I know I've been a bitch
but Tom's . . .'

'Ruined everything?'
she finishes for me.

I look out of the window
stare at the sky, rubbing my eyes,
searching for words.

'You know,' Hannah says,
lifting Martha on to her hip,

Tabitha happily graffiting the wall
where her little sister left off,
'you don't have to stay with him,
he's not so much of a catch,
Emma, let's be frank' –
(she covers Martha's ears)
– 'he's a bit of a cunt.'

I laugh.
At you,
with her,
betraying everything we are
without a moment's guilt.


## HUSBAND

Hannah gives me your other women,
their names and dates,
reminding me again how good you are at betrayal.

She describes the blemishes and stains
that salt couldn't lift,
the threadbare lies, and lack.

She implies that you took things
she didn't want to give,
years of her life wasted on yours.

She throws me your indifference
to your children and
her work.

Hannah gives me your excuses
and then she laughs,

as she gives me your protestations of
blamelessness,

and laughs again

when she tells me I did her a favour in the end.


**ADVICE**

Tentative, I wonder
what she thinks I should do.

She shrugs,
'I mean, of course, Tom's brilliant –
in many ways.
It depends on what you're prepared to tolerate.

I think he was always more in love with himself
than he ever was with me
and there are limits, Emma,
to what you can give.
In fact I don't think we should even be talking in terms
of sacrifice.
Love's not that.'

I mumble that she's right
and want to beg her for her recipe
for survival,
the trick of confidence.

I itch to tell her everything,
to ask her
to fix me,
but know
she owes me nothing more.

Hannah marshals the girls,
expert, efficient,
she didn't touch her coffee,
didn't even sit beside me,
and before I can ask her to stay, they've gone.
I tell myself I don't want to be her friend
anyway.

Upstairs,
I drag out the suitcase I've half packed,
stare at the choice:
leave you
or stay
and enact some sort of revenge.

I've read them all,
the stories of retribution
and it never ends well.

And you have never needed anyone's approval,
will do what you have always done.

Is there any point in starting a war
I can't win?


## RESEARCH

I sit in a corner of a coffee shop
where I won't be seen
and turn on my laptop,
plug in the device
that I stole from your bag and
face up to the facts.

There are files and files of work.

You keep your life on here,
I realize,
pictures of your daughters,
sweet,
and your eyes are kind
as you look down at them
with paternal pride.

Not many photos of me.
Of us.
More of my body
than there are of my face.

And then there are your poems
that I glance through
cursorily,
dismissing them
as quickly as I'd dismiss my own.

You've never shared your work,
as if my opinion is not worth
hearing;
of course you are beyond my understanding.

I open up a folder called
*New Mew*
(you cheeky fuck)
and read the correspondence copied there,
the offer of publication,
the book slated for autumn this year –

and I'm seeing that future
on my screen,
like a movie playing out:
the reviews, the launch,
friends and colleagues lauding you,
queueing up to glorify you –
how you'll wash, shave and preen yourself

handsome for the event
rather than show up your true self.

And once we've toasted you
and your book,
laughed and marvelled
at the extent of your genius,

once you've published my work
under your name,

what then?
What's the plan?

Do you think that perhaps then you'll set me back on
     track?
Writing, thinking, researching,
a version of Milton's daughter,
and you the
tyrant father
going blind,
epic exploiter, demeaner,
forcing words into your daughter's hands.

And your own children, you won't see what they need
although if you'd listened
then perhaps you'd have heard
the confession of a murderous plan
to slaughter you in your sleep,
to roast your heart
and eat it.
Maybe if you weren't such an egotist
you'd get the message that there
is no love left.

I search the manuscript,
assess what you've done.
It isn't complete by any means,

the last chapters
just as lean as I left them,
the traces of your greedy fingers
there in the occasional bored annotation.

So when's this book getting finished then?

I wonder what you think I'll do
and what my role is now to be.

You appear oblivious to the idea
that you've been found out
and I wonder when it will sink in
that I haven't stayed with you for fun.

You don't seem to have considered
how exactly I will be paid
for acquiescing to your plan.

Perhaps you will offer me
morsels of your soul in return
for my whole self.

Maybe you imagine there will be a deal,
a pact,
and I, so desperate for your touch,
will sit patiently
as you set about me
with a trepanning tool,
let you
perforate my skull
and remove
the portions of brain
that might be of use.

Maybe you will eat them
with fava beans and a nice Chianti.

I hide my smile behind my hand,
swallow the joke
into my belly
and suffer the rumble of it
mixing with the acid indigestion,
the wave of nausea that swells
every time I think of you
stealing my work,
because it isn't nice to be a victim.

It is a murder I wake up to
every day.


## WORKSHOP

You used to talk me through my writing.
School me on the use of imagery,
show me where my metaphors mixed
or failed to express an idea
originally.

You picked me apart
that first year
we lived together,
when I should have been basking
in my new-found fame,
performing at festivals, even Hay,
new ideas spilling over fresh white pages,
and working out who I was
rather than beginning to doubt
that any of it
was good enough.

We workshopped me
just for fun.

The more whisky you drank
the clearer it became
that you were laughing at the new work I'd done.

*Rather derivative,*
you said,
kindly, of course,
patting my knee,
*too much Plath* –
'Honestly, Em,
I don't want to make you feel bad.
But hasn't it been done?
All this confessional stuff?
It's just a bit self-indulgent.
The work needs to be
a lot more
robust.'

And I felt myself relegated,
third division –
maybe not even that,
maybe just out of the game
for good.
I was twenty-two
and I thought I'd broken in,
found the code,
picked the lock.

I took my poems back,
staggered, heart reeling,
held the manuscript to my chest
so you wouldn't see it bleeding
and I felt ashamed
of the words I'd written down on those pages
because what you'd scorned was
my soul,
my self.

There has to be a cost,
a fine
for vandalizing what I was.
I was just beginning
when you cocked your leg and pissed
on my
newly painted promise
and convinced me
that I was the fake.


## LOVE BOMB

You call, invite me for dinner,
and I suspect there is an ulterior motive
although you say nothing
about your missing memory stick –
perhaps you've done the sensible thing
and backed everything up.

I doubt it.

'I have plans,' I tell you.
There's a pause –
it's not the response you wanted
or anticipated.

'That's a shame.' You're cautious and
I can feel persuasion coming on,
a rolling tide of sweetness
that I fortify myself against by speaking
up quickly, ensuring you understand.

'Yes, I'm seeing Ari –
we're going to a play.'

No lie.
'Something experimental,

a new drama,
a one-woman
show.'

I could invite
you along.
I don't. But you're
home in time to see me go –

you compliment my hair
my clothes.
Hold on to my hand
for longer than is necessary,
kiss my neck.
'Do you really have to go out?
I bought fresh fish
and your favourite wine,
I'll cook you supper
and we'll talk?'

'Sorry, I'm running late.'
I kiss you as I back away
so you won't suspect,
and
wonder how long my body will
lie for me –
wonder when my stomach will start to rebel,
if I might retch
at the touch of your hands on my skin,
if I will shiver, shudder,
revolted,
later when your beard
grates my chin.

If I'll bleed all over the bed.

Resisting the itch to scratch,
I touch your face, say,

'You should shave,'
and leave you alone with your fish and the thought of
whatever else it is you planned to take
from me tonight.


## ICONOCLAST

Could you call that a victory?
I'm not sure
if I humbled you,
made you aware that you are not
everything to me any more
and that actually
I have rumbled you.

Perhaps it's because I don't believe
in the myth,
because I've destroyed the image I had
of you in my head
now you've smashed the sacred artefacts
of our love.

I want you to know that
I know that
you're not who you pretend to be.
Nothing has been forgotten.

Ariel hugs me,
slings his arm over my shoulder, and
we walk towards the theatre
talking, talking, talking.

'Did you tell the prof?' he asks.
'I thought he might come,
I know Jaz would have been chuffed.'

'Sorry, he was busy,
said maybe next time
with a bit more warning.'
How easily I tell lies –
it's because you and I are
hiders and seekers
who never tell a truth
if a subterfuge will do –

but I don't want to be that way any more,
so I pause
and then tell Ariel the truth:
that I didn't invite you,
we're having problems,
and it would have been awkward.
'I'm sorry,
please forgive me.'

Ariel doesn't seem to care, shrugs,
says he's sorry to hear it's not going well,
frowns and asks,
'Are you OK?'
And suddenly I'm not.

It all comes back.
how little I have,
and that there is still no plan.

All the bluster and bullshit
that I'm fighting back and will bundle you
wholesale out of my life
is crap.

I'm standing in the foyer
making a scene,
surrounded by people who are noticing me
weeping and carrying on,
telling this man I barely know

that I'm not all right –
'But thank you for asking –
I haven't really slept.
I'm probably just tired.
Ignore me,
look, let's just go in and sit down.'

Ari grabs me, holds me,
folds me up tight,
and I like the feeling of his strength,
his smell,
my face right up against
the soft pale blue of his chest.
I breathe in kindness and like its sweet taste.

We sit outside the theatre,
watch people stream inside,
and I tell him that it's falling apart –
you and me –
that you've done something awful,
there's been a terrible betrayal.
I make it sound like an affair.
Ariel holds my hand, makes sympathetic noises,
says he totally understands.

I'm allowed to be angry,
Ariel says,
about everything –
'You have the right to rage, Emma.'
The tears on my face
are a manifestation of the way I feel, he says –
'It's good to be real.'

Still I swipe them away
and try to smile.
'Now you just look crazy,' he says.
And I laugh through the snot,
spewing swear words and then revealing,
'I keep thinking how I could hurt him back.'

Ari considers, as if mulling over how this might work.
'What's his Achilles heel?' he asks,
fascinated by the idea that his prof might be weak.

'I know what I'd like to expose.'

'Go on,' Ari says,
hanging off my words,
so I speak in code,
relishing the taste of revenge on my tongue –
hot salt and spice, its sour tang.
'Well, if everyone knew
what a fraud he is . . .'

'You mean you think
you'd transfer your pain on to him?'

Whatever.
I rant about you.
How people should know the kind of man
you really are,
a cheater, a liar, an absolute prick.

'You shouldn't suffer,' Ari says gently,
relishing my hate
but watching me
in a way that makes me want to claw out his eyes.

Does he think I'll start a physical fight?
Wild in the quad, with my nails to your face and
my fist in your gut?
I know how that would work out.

And wouldn't they all be satisfied to see me sink so low,
reverting to type: savage little oik.
Crude fishwife.

'You're not going to do anything rash, though, Em?
I mean, I reckon it could get nasty
if you go for him.'

'Why shouldn't I?
He deserves it,
he's screwed me over
and he'll do it again
to someone else –
in fact, he already has.'

And now he's considering,
as if he's taking me seriously,
but eventually he shakes his head,
too reasonable for a man of twenty-three.

'OK, but listen –
I don't know, would you actually feel better?
Could be bad karma somewhere down the line.'

Cowardly, he wavers –
but I don't want to ratiocinate,
don't want to be rinsed clean of my rage
because then
what will be left?

'Probably, yeah.
Yes, I think I would feel better.'

'So leave him.
If he makes you miserable,
I don't get why you'd stay?'


## EXODUS

Leave with what?
Go where?

I have nothing,
can't retreat to my parents' –
how would I explain?
I can imagine their faces:
beyond confused, and sad too,
that I've had to concede
I wasn't clever enough, after all.

No. Defeat is not the solution.
I will not retreat.

Ari's ideas come at me,
practicalities, emotions
that complicate my plans:
that Tom would suffer,
and maybe *he's not such a bad bloke,*
*remember, Tom's a bloody good teacher,*
*who a lot of students love.*
He's not sure people would believe me
or even care that much.

'It's not like people don't cheat.
Monogamy is an illusion, right?'

I pull my hand from his
and walk ahead, hurrying
into the night.

But he follows me,
talking – perhaps he thinks that it helps.
'Maybe you can get a room in college
or a shared house –
accommodation is available outside walls for post-grads –
come on, Em, you can hustle,
do your own thing.
You're strong. You've got this. Right?'

I don't tell Ari about my debts,
that I have no money,

that I have wasted months
doing nothing.
That I rely on you to feed me,
to keep me,
that I take coins from your wallet,
notes from your desk
and resent
your parsimony nevertheless.

A thought worms under my skin
and moves up my veins,
grows fatter and thicker,
coils tight at my neck.
I scratch and cough,
choking on it –

standing still
in the street
in the traffic –

confronting the monstrous truth
that perhaps
you've earned my work.

It's payback for all the times
you've bailed me out,
paid a credit card bill,
crossly telling me I need to get a grip,
get a job,
make some money,
that you're not my dad
or NatWest bloody bank.

You have no room to talk:
your mother's family money
keeps you afloat.

But what contribution have I made
to the running of our household

other than dead poems
and a half-finished thesis?
A few loaves of bread made,
shopping,
cleaning your toilet,
planting flowers which never grew?

No wonder you're bored,
angry,
frustrated.
No wonder you don't rate me.


~


We forget the show.
Tonight I don't think I can face
watching people pretend to be
something they're not.
Ari takes my hand and leads me
to the bus
and I sit silently
while he talks and I nod, agreeing with
everything and nothing.

He cooks student food –
pasta and pesto
stirred in the pan,
served on to our laps
on mismatching plates –
and he feeds me chocolate, cheap, strong red wine,
waits for me to talk to him
as if I'll have something interesting to say
but I am zeroed,
blank –

out of complaints.

I don't want to entertain
anyone with stories of your cruelty.
I don't want him probing any further into us.

If you were here
you wouldn't be thinking of me,
you'd be in another room
with someone more interesting.
I have seen it in your face –
that I am dull;
I have outlived my interest
and am only surviving on usefulness.

There's an irony in there somewhere,
but I'm too stupid to work it out.
An analogy is easier;
if I were an ornament
I'd be relegated to the cellar
or taken to the charity shop.

You are sick of looking at me
and the feeling is mutual.
I can't go home
ever again.

'Can I stay?' I ask Ari.
He nods, not looking surprised,
and I don't ask where he plans to put me.
If it's in his bed then
OK, whatever, I think –
he doesn't need to touch me.

But later, when we lie
close,
skin to skin,
I kiss him,
he kisses me,
and I'm watching us

from the ceiling
staring down at my body
having sex with someone
I barely know
and
I'm glad when it's over.

Men sleep
and women lie awake in the darkness thinking
of what it must be like
not to be rendered sleepless
with self-doubt.

My legs itch with blood
and the urge to run away from Ariel
and his bed.
I stare wide-eyed at the walls
and try not to scratch
and imagine you
blistered all over and
boiling in a vat
of your own piss.

Are you missing me?
Are you sad
that I haven't come home?
Do you think you've won
or are you afraid
of what I might do now?

∽

My phone wakes me
after too little sleep,
ringtone a whistle.
I am being
catcalled, beckoned –

by you, Tom, on the other end of the line.

'Where are you?
Why didn't you come home?'

Abrupt, foul mood,
you are rude
and I don't have my 'because' ready,
have run out of ways to tell you
what you have done to me

and I've been wondering if after all
I'm sure
that I want to be here,
in Ari's room.

Pleasure is
measured in morsels that
taste of ashes,
fingernails, hair,
all the muck
that collects under the bed.
The filth of it is lodged between my legs.

(Oh God, the ways I make mistakes.)

'Why are you calling me?
Why do you care?'
I snap back, and the silence you give me is
a sweet-smelling gas
invading the room and I sink back
into the bed,
close my eyes,
breathing as you breathe,
left to interpret atoms
invisible molecules of thought –

it is all
beyond words.

'I'm going into college,' you say
eventually.
'Why don't you meet me later
in town.'

Ari is waking, watching me,
and I turn to face the wall,
hide the evidence
that I can't
entirely leave you –
I didn't need to pick up this call
but I suppose I wanted to hear your voice.

'I don't think so,' I say.

'OK, well, will you be home later?'
The thought that you want me
to be there
is another
sign
that I have to remind myself not to interpret
as something that it is not.

Instead I focus on the tone of your voice,
a little intrigued,
but mostly annoyed.

I look at Ari's pit of a room –
small, the bed not designed for two –
think of the bed I share with you.

The sheets I chose,
my clothes
hanging – his and hers –
nestled in drawers,
curving and curling into yours.

Swinging my legs out of the bed,
I walk to the window,

open it,
lean out, away,
breathe in the fresh air, shiver in the rain,
say,
'OK, maybe. I'll see –
I'm not sure what I'm doing yet.
I'm thinking about leaving you, Tom,
but I need to come back, get my things.
I'll stay with a friend while I work out what's next.'

'Leaving me?'

'Yes.
It's for the best, right?
Don't you think?'

It isn't the time or place to have this
conversation,
my timing is off,
as usual.

Ari is pretending not to listen
but I don't blame him,
turn to face him,
let him see
what this is doing to me,
that it's not as easy as it sounds.

Maybe he mistakes the rain on my face
for tears
because he gets up,
holds me,
kisses my neck,
runs his hands over my arms, my breasts –

I suppose I hang up.

We go back to bed.

Sleepwalking fingers creep and crawl.
An invasion that has no interest in words.

I can't explain
the situation again,
and Ari doesn't ask me to.

'Stay,' he says.


## MISSION

The imperative is getting revenge;
not allowing this, or running away.

I drink coffee so fast it burns my mouth,
thinking –
how can I hurt you most?

I will find your weak spot
and press it with my thumbs,
push so hard
you'll burst.

You've got me already,
know my Achilles heel –

and I am held by it now,
twisting upside down, strung up
like a chicken
in a butcher's shop,
slaughtered and plucked.

You don't think I'll dare to say a word.

All night it's roiled in my belly
the knowledge that you think you've won.

So.

I swig the coffee
and go.

The house is silent and still
and the garden white with frost,
the earth too hard and unyielding
to stop here
where you are not.

Wearing yesterday's clothes,
I walk to your college;
straight through the gates,
no one stops me –

I look like a student.
I am a student.
I have the right to step on to this grass
should I so choose.

The door to your office is closed.
I grab the handle and
stand, holding on –
perhaps you have a tutorial,
I check your schedule on my phone
and do what I should have done in the first place –
just walk in.

But you look like you've been expecting me.
I can't surprise you
or take you by the roots and shake you
out of your complacence.

I bore you.
Predictable, so unoriginal.

Well. Just you wait.

Your eyes drift,
ashy with ennui,
although the students
sitting opposite you
in the midst of their tutorial
are staring at me like I might have a gun
or a knife,
a scorned woman
on the rampage – perhaps it's happened before.

So I almost leave
before I can accuse you of anything.

Because I always try to be polite
when I can.

'Emma? Can I help?
Is everything all right?'

Smooth,
oiling the room with feigned surprise,
you smile.

God, that smile
is such a lie.

You know fine rightly
that nothing whatsoever is fine.

'Tom, so sorry to interrupt,
I thought I'd come and let you know
I'm on my way to Margaret Browning's office now –
I'm going to tell her what you've done,
I was thinking perhaps you'd like to come along?'

You don't move.
Not even a twitch.

The students stare,
look from you to me.

I focus – take in the girl,
who could be a first year, perhaps,
or second,
I've seen her around.
Was she at ours at New Year?
One of your groupies?
I imagine she's easily
impressed by everything you say,
scribbling down
your words,
barely pausing
when you announce
that Emily Brontë is awfully irritating.

'What are you working on?' I ask her.
'Is it Victorians this term,
or maybe twentieth century?
Is he teaching you Browning, or Yeats?'
I grab her essay out of her hands
and begin to read something about
tragic joy – death transformed into
ecstasy at the end.
'God, the poets know, don't they?
They get it right time and time again
and we don't listen, don't take any notice.
I should have seen this coming,
it's fucking rote.'

I thrust back the essay
and she tries to catch the papers
but they flutter
disordered to the floor
and I laugh again
at the symbolism.

A book about Tom Abbot and irony
would have been so easy
to write.

You could make it your next piece,
maybe I'll suggest it,
set you up with another nice little premise.

I pace the room,
run my hand over your magnificent desk
where you lifted me,
naked,
the windows wide open to the air.
I never thought about the eyes
that might spot us,
didn't care what I did
or how much noise we made.

I stand on the patch of rug where I knelt
once
or twice
and shake my head at the memory of my desire
of how I wanted you
to do
anything to me,

how I would have done
anything for you.

I mutter how
I liked it.
I loved it.

I loved you.
'Remember, Tom?'

'Emma –'
You're up, out of your chair at last,

hand on my arm,
gesturing at the students
while you try to
calm me down.

But I don't want to be calm.
You don't deserve peace.
You deserve to be served
dishes of malice garnished with thorns.

'Is everything all right?
You seem to be in a bit of a state.
Let me take you home –
we'll get you sorted out.'

'Get your hands off me,
*Tom*,
I'm fine.'

I step back, holding up my palms –
ready and armed
with your secrets.

I look at the girl again,
aim my words at her,
spittle flying, finger stabbing:
'Just watch out –
he'll act like everything you've ever thought is his.'

I tell the room that
I thought you meant it when you told me
I had          potential, was          beautiful and     clever.

'Sorry,' I throw up my hands,
'but it's all just lies.'

Why don't these students
do something?

Why don't they call the police?
Shout and scream on my behalf?

I wonder what Margaret Browning will say
when she hears of this?

My mind runs forward to the moment I crack you open
and the rot starts spilling,
covering her floor, our feet, our clothes,
and my jaw aches
with the words I have chewed
over all night and now spit out.

You speak,
pianissimo,
no hint of the boiling rage
I can smell on your breath.
'I'm sorry – Lois, Stephen, you'd better leave.
We'll come back to this another day.'

The room spins
and I need to sit because
somehow I'm failing,
dissolving in the face of your control.

It wasn't supposed to be this way.

You were supposed to admit it,
say sorry,
beg me for mercy.

So I don't understand why
I've faded to the floor
and you haven't even flinched.

The door closes behind them,
leaving me alone with you.

You look down at me, raise an eyebrow,
watching me,
and I curse my legs that lack the strength
to run
when you lean in,
and spray my face:

'Have you lost your fucking mind?
What is this, Emma? Ambushing me here,
in college, in front of students,
my place of work.
Are you insane?'

'It's not me,' I hiss,
'it's you.
I know what you're up to, Tom.
I know about the book.
*My* work.
I know about everything you've done.'

'What? Come on now.
This is absurd.
I thought we'd gone through this.
What exactly are you accusing me of today?'

I repeat it.
That you're a thief and a pig.

You tap your finger on my forehead.
'I don't think so, darling.
What's yours is mine, yes?
You wouldn't be here if it weren't for me.
I led you like a donkey
and showed you where to go,
how to explore, use your brain –
in fact, I'd say, and I think it's fair,
I taught you how to think
when you came here,
that silly little girl without a single idea of her own.

And it's nothing extraordinary,
for Christ's sake: we're not splitting the atom.
You were just researching
a dead poet.
That's all she is.
Haven't you got the message yet
that no one gives a shit?'

You wait for my reaction,
taking off my skin with each syllable
flaying me with your words
and I cower,
can't help but give you
my fear.

You grip my arms,
hold my face.
'Do you realize how many copies I'll actually sell?
No one will read it –
no one gives a damn.'

You bark out a laugh.
'You've forgotten I have an ex-wife
and two daughters to fund.
Parasites, the lot of you.'

How can it mean so little?
Be so insignificant?
How can you tell me that it stands for nothing?

Maybe to you
it's just a boast,
another little book on a shelf.
Proof to your college that you're doing your work.

Or perhaps you've perceived
that the time is right
for a man to come out hollering,

raising up a forgotten voice;
will you fashion yourself as an ally to our rage?

Maybe you want to speak for us,
over us,
into us,
skin me and stitch a megaphone
out of my hide.

Or maybe you just want to do a bit more TV,
have something new to tweet.


## MARGARET BROWNING

You drop me.
Move to the desk, pick up the telephone
and make a call,
summoning someone, saying,
'Yes, please, if you have a minute,
can you come?
I'd appreciate it.'

Who are you calling?
The proctor?
The police?

But it's Margaret Browning
who stands in the doorway.
Her shoes are purple,
her tights bright pink.
I look up at her
from the floor,
then stand up,
straighten out the ache and twist
of my face.

'Tom? Emma?
How can I help?'

You gesture that I should speak
and sit back in your chair,
arms folded, legs crossed, your face a study of
bemusement.
And I stutter my way towards
Margaret, my explanations so pitiful
that she stops me when I'm not even halfway done
telling the story of your
subterfuge –
I lean against the desk,
legs trembling too much
to hold me up
the room is quivering, crumbling, books
falling;
an avalanche of grammar –
complex sentences wallop and whack,
and I am buried under a rush of full stops.
Slashed into pieces by subordinate clauses.
Stifled by epilogues.

I cover my ears,
my face,
my head.
Want to shrink,
maggot small, and crawl
away from her questions which come unabated.
Her forehead creases.
'I'm sorry, Emma, I'm not sure I understand.
What's happened?
Is it your work?
Can't you get someone from I.T. to take a look?
I'm not sure what it is that you want?'

Margaret frowns, looks at Tom,
not trying to disguise her disbelief:

it sounds like the dog-ate-my-homework kind of crap –
I know she gets all sorts from undergrads
and she'll think this is more of the same,
that I'm stalling,
finding reasons not to come through.
She towers above me
as I try to explain –

'Sorry, I don't think I'm being clear.
Not lost, Margaret.' I lean up,
supplicating, begging, whispering.
I stand, speak close to her ear.
'Stolen.'

'What? How can someone have stolen your ideas?
I'm sorry, Emma, I'm not sure I follow.
Are you saying that the work you've undertaken
for the past four years
has now just vanished?'

She snaps her fingers
like a magician miming disappearance.

'Yes.'
(*It's Tom.*
*He's taken it all.*)
The accusation
is in my eyes
my fists
my nails
that crave to score you open
paint your bleeding entrails
all over this room.

'Tom?'
She looks back at you.
Unspoken words pass,
the sizzle of synapses
the firing of thoughts.

You clear your throat, get up and
crouch down beside me,
make a show of
trying to help me to my feet.

'Emma's had a hard few months,
what with the miscarriage, you know, and whatnot.
If you could reassure her,
Margaret, that all will be well,
that she will find her way back to herself,
it might help us to
put together some sort of plan.'

The subtext is of course:
how dare I have the temerity to presume
that I could ever be as good as you.
Better if I accept your version of me:
weak, vulnerable,
quite possibly
in need of a lunatic's cell.

It is harder than I'd imagined
to get Margaret to understand,
and I'm shouting and wrestling myself out of your arms
away from your hands
that are so big
one could span my neck
or crush my skull.
I stand up straight and face Margaret
dead on.

'He stole my work,
my chapters,
everything I've done.'

But it's a muddle,
like a paintbrush
dragged from one colour to the next

I blur the edges
mess up the page
tear the paper
and my hair.

'Emma,' she tells me,
'you're not making sense.'

Believing me relies on believing that you
are a charlatan
a mountebank
a cheat

and I'm not sure she's there yet.

'I'm sorry, Margaret—'
I try to breathe,
regret calling you a cunt
and making her think I've lost
more than my work.

I should have shown up
wearing something smart and a smile,
spoken in smooth measured tones,
not arrived after a night screwing another bloke
clothes creased
face smudged
with lack of sleep
stink of sex still on my breath
and more words for bastard than you can count.

I should have made an appointment,
written it all out – nice and neat.
We should have sat around a table,
I could have made my case,
left her in no doubt
that I was perfectly sane.

But as it is, no one believes me.

I gather my bag,
straighten my clothes,
my face,
and button my coat
to catch my flailing heart inside.

I leave them,
the air
        still heaving
with the panic of birds trapped
in a windowless space
hurling themselves against walls.


## LOST

Walking helps,
then running fast,
the thud of the street under my feet –
its solidity
reminds me that there are facts

and I need to get mine straight.

Throwing wild accusations –
as you would call them,
as you did call them –
will get me nowhere.

Games of hide-and-seek as a child when
I lay under a bed, covered in dust,
giggling,
giving myself away,
or cheating in tests –
French vocab written under a sleeve
and the teacher almost laughing
at my pathetic attempt to hide:

he could see
right through me.

Naive fool
to think that in this place,
this ancient town
of towers and walls,
my voice might fall
on listening ears.

I stop and stare at stone,
rest my forehead on the cold,
shut my eyes and breathe in the brick.
I'd bite it if my teeth wouldn't smash,
would gnaw my way
into the marrow of these buildings,
ingesting their power.

No one stops.
No one sees
me standing there
haunted by my poet's mad Ken
with his eyes like wounds –
red stars, Charlotte called them –
how as he walked he held his hands before him
braced against the threat of bars.

Have I stepped inside her poem?
My own face feels raw
my eyes bleed shame
as if I have been flayed
nerves pulped
meat hooked.
Is that what you want?

I glance over my shoulder
afraid of who might have slipped into my shadow,
who it is that might be tracking me,

my phone chirrups –
Ari.

I find my way to town and the bustle of shops,
cafes, light and life.
A strange normality
I cannot adjust myself to fit.
We drink tea
and my legs shake.
I fidget in my seat,
spilling sugar and salt,
mixing them on the table top
drawing lines
fences
locked boxes
curbs and bolts and bars
then sitting on my hands to stop
the itch of anxiety,
the compulsion to worry
that this is it –
I'm

(un)done.

'Why don't you tell me everything.'
Ari watches me,
hand twitching as if he'd like to reach and still
my frantic fingers.
'It might help.'
And then he waits for a decent response.
I suppose I should be grateful
that's he's reaching out.

When I shrug he presses on,
'What precisely has the prof done?
It can't be that bad, surely –
I mean, look at us, last night.
It can't have been much worse than that.

Has he actually been having a full-on affair?
Is that why you're so upset?'

I stare him down,
ask what he knows.

Maybe there's another woman as well,
and Ari's just a lad keeping lads' secrets –
some private members' club.

He freezes at the accusation, draws back,
afraid of muddying his lovely life with my mess.
And if my tone suggested that I think he's complicit,
well, he wouldn't believe me if I told him the facts,
so in that sense
he is.

I can already hear him defend you
tell me that his *prof* is no plagiarist –
certainly no thief.
Oh, yes, Ariel would accuse me of
imagining ridiculous things.

He holds up his hands.
'Look, don't ask me,
it's not as if we're mates,
he's my supervisor, and I rate him
and as far as I know he's a bloody good bloke,
but I'm worried. Look, Emma, are you OK?
You don't look so great.'

'God, yes, fine – all right,
forget it, please, I don't want to talk about it,
it's a waste of time.'

'Course.
Look, if it's that bad
why don't you stay with me for a while,
you can share my room, decide what's next.'

He covers my hand at last
and I don't move,
don't reciprocate the affection,
don't feel anything right this second.

Numb,
as if I am matchstalk-made:
washed-out watercolour, ivory and black,
in a place I thought I'd left behind,
shunted right back
to where I began.
My lips
split on the thought
and I'm spitting tea,
choking on my inability to tell him
what it means to have failed.

'Look, Ari,' I begin,
'I mean, you're lovely and everything
but I can't move in with you –
not like that –
I'm going to have to leave,
maybe go back home.'

I can't. I won't.
I know this is a lie
to get me out of
becoming that girl again,
reliant on some man
who doesn't understand.

'And where's that?'

'Far away from here.
This place.
Where everyone is so full of bull –
you know it means nothing, Ari, right?
Whether you're good at it or not,

whether you get the grade,
write a book,
in the real world no one actually cares.
This place, it's monstrous,
it gobbles you up.'

I'm rambling
but I know there's a truth in this.
I sit there
banging my chest with my fist
as nonsense ricochets from wall to wall;
childish, I complain
about injustice
and say,
*It's not fair*, over and over again.

But my voice must be too loud
because I hear it coming back to me:
shrill echo,
shrieking complaints,
making accusations of foul play.

Ari backs away,
pays the bill,
steers me
outside
and I bend over
hands on my knees.

'Sorry,' I tell him, panting words,
'I'll be fine.
Need some time
to decide
what I'm going to do.
Please, Ari, go –
don't worry
best if you just leave me alone.'

He walks away
and I pull what is left of myself together
again.

I blame you, Tom,
for this.

If you come for me again,
try to unpick me
and make me bleed,
lie that you never lied to me,
smile serenely
as you button my lips
and tie me up in paradox

I don't know what I'll do.


## PERPETUAL MOTION

If I shut my eyes I can see it coming:

Here are the walls.
And here
you are racing towards me.

And there I am

                                        darting away
                        and back again
turning
                and turning
in terrible circles

trapped and waiting
                                        for someone
to slip,      tripped
                and stumbling, not sure

what it is                                        they're chasing.

What if it's me who falls?

What if you catch me
and you're wearing your armour
and you put your lips to my palm.

What if I drop back into your arms
and open my veins?

⌒

The sun comes out
and I sit on the stone steps beside the Sheldonian
listening to an orchestra tuning up,
the drum of the Radcliffe Camera beating behind me,
watching the world and waiting,
thinking about burning things down.
Flames catch in my throat
as I begin to suffocate
on the idea of destroying the place.
I wrote it in my diary,
aged just fifteen:
go to Oxford,
be something,
be better
than me.

And now here I am
sitting in a winter sun
that doesn't touch me, rays out of reach,
because I was never bright enough to see
the way it worked.

I thought it ended when I'd only just begun.
One book of poems,
and the man I thought
would make me
something.
That was my mistake right there,

the oldest one
there is.

I wanted to sit in a book-lined room
wombed in words.
I didn't see the tomb that waited
for the woman
who underrated herself.


## GO, LEAVE

I sit in the kitchen
in my coat,
bag at my feet,
waiting.

On the table is the memory stick
I stole.

I watch it
and realize how pitiful
to think
I had you
with that –

what proof?

You are late
and it's dark,
very, very dark,
and I am very, very still,
sitting here
aching.

You turn on the light
and startle
when you see me.

But you don't speak.

You go about your business
as if I am not here,
that game we play –
childish:
who will speak first
prove they still care,
acknowledge that there was once
love?
But now it's
dying here in front of us.
At least a word would mean
you want
to pick it up
and resuscitate our corpse.

You pour yourself a glass of water,
leave the room
and close your study door.


## MARYANNE

I call her from the bar
where I'm crouched
over my glass.

I took the money for my drink from your drawer
where you leave coppers, coins
and the detritus of your life.

On the phone she sounds so far away
and too much has happened for me to explain –

'Emma, what's wrong?'

The noise of the pub throws my words away from her
and all I have is tears.

'Can I come?' I ask, my voice thick and faint.
'But I don't have money –
can you help?'

'What? Why?
Are you leaving Tom?'

'I'm trying to.'

The bag at my feet full of
pants, bras,
pyjamas,
stuffed and rolled clothes,
a bar of soap
and some of that make-up
I never used.

'I need to start again.
Please,
can I come and stay with you?'

Helplessness making me sick,
I drain my drink
and wish she'd just say, *Yes.*
*Here's a ticket.*
*Hurry, I'm here, waiting* –
but she is telling me that she's going to be away,
a holiday
with a new man
and that she can't cancel it –
but maybe if I were to wait a week or two?
When she gets back
she'll sort it for me
and in the meantime
how about she sends me a hundred quid?

She'll do a bank transfer later today
but she's rushing for a meeting.

Doesn't she realize
I'm skint?

Has she forgotten what it is
to be
in deep shit?

The pub closes and I walk.
Night-time
and nowhere to go.

A voice tells me to get a grip, to go home.
You? My dad? My mum?
So melodramatic, someone says.

Strap of my bag cutting into my shoulder,
feet slow and tired of walking,
worn out with running, bones aching
here on St Aldate's, in the dark, walking towards the river.
A man on a bike slows and I tense
as he circles back.
He stops. Asks if I'm all right.

I thank him, walk away as if I have a destination,
pull out my phone again and dial a number
that I used once before when I was new here,
my first term,
first time away from home
and, even despite her, my poet, so alone.

The kind, calm voice on the other end of the line waits
to give me anonymous advice.
I breathe and wonder –
what can I say?

I hang up before he has the chance
to find out
how he can help.

☙

Ariel takes me in.

Better to have a bed
even if I have to share with him.

Better to have sex
than to die
alone
out there.

## MADNESS

You always told me there was a chance
I'd become just like her,
Charlotte Mew.
Suicidal poet.

'You're obsessed, Emma,' you said,
'and it's a good thing
in many ways,
but to identify quite so closely
with your subject
is possibly a little unhealthy.'

I think about how my Charlotte took her life
alone, in a room without a view,
believing she'd be better off dead
than alive and mad.
I stare at the blue bottle of bleach by Ari's toilet,

lift it
        shake it
                almost        empty
not enough here to do the job –
it would just be another terrible mess.

The thought makes me retch
and scores my throat
as I throw up bile.

Ari is watching me when I open my eyes
his face too close.

'What happened, then?' he wants to know,
so I admit that I've left you
and had nowhere else.
'Thanks for taking me in,' I tell him
as his hand strokes my stomach and my breasts,
and my face, lips, tongue
give him the proof of my gratitude.


## WORDS

At least I'm writing.
The consolation in despair:
poetry –
like a monster waiting to tear out of its cave
the moment you begin
to fail.

Lines roar from my pen.

I sit in a patch of January sun
outside the Sheldonian
at my post,
my lookout,

watching for the storm
that's growling somewhere
just beyond the city's walls.

My bag of things at my feet
and notebook on my knee
I am
writing
writing
writing

mostly about you.

Maybe I'll thank you one day
for giving me something new to say.

You pushed, just one idle finger applied to my chest,
and I fell
head over heels, grit in my eyes and rocks in my back,
until, spreadeagled and screaming,
I landed here.
And I can't climb back up.
Not that way, your way.
I don't speak that language any more.

I press the aches one by one
to remind myself of what you've done.

Then,
'Excuse me?'
Polite. Uncertain. A girl's voice –
I look at her,
don't recognize for a moment
the mirror cracking
as I see myself
seven years ago in Lois,
the kid from your room,

yesterday, only yesterday,
the tutorial I wrecked.
Does she want to shout at me?
Maybe she wants to tell me I let her down,
let them all down,
by failing to go ahead with my life –
to move on,
forward march,
pave a clear path to the top.

'Sorry, um – so, hi –
I just wanted to check,
are you OK?'
She is nice. Of course she is.
It's only you and I who struggle with that.

I tell her I'm completely fine,
that I'm sorry about what happened.
'It was one of those days.'

I try to project maturity,
adulthood,
tame the wildness, twist my hair
around my hand, stand up and
adjust my bag on my shoulder,
straighten myself
and shake catastrophe out of my face.
I wish I could fold myself into a clean, neat square
and tidy myself quietly away.

'I know it must have looked odd' –
I cough and blush –
'but actually' –
I touch my cheek,
burning hot –
'I'm good.
Please, could you just forget it?'
I laugh at myself, willing her to join in.
'Just pretend it never happened?'

'Oh OK.
It's just,
if you've got a minute,
I wondered if we could talk.'

She pauses and looks around.
Traffic of tourists,
streams of them
ebb and flow around us,
and I know it's safe to say anything at all,
no one is listening –
certainly not these ancient walls
that creak with the secrets of centuries
far more important than ours.

Of course you, Tom, don't want to give this place up,
you live for its kudos.
All of us,
any of us,
would do anything to stay
here.
Special, chosen, gilded.

I need to get over this.

Lois interrupts,
anxious, waiting for a response.
'If you're not busy,
could we maybe go somewhere private,
not out here?'

Of course she doesn't want to be seen
talking to me,
doesn't want to be observed by you
or some snitch,
and it's true:
you could emerge at any moment
out of the Bodleian,

jog over here
and ask us
what the hell is going on.

You could accuse me of trying to corrupt
poor Lois,
to sour her mind.
She is right to be afraid of
the consequences
of associating with someone like me,
as I should have been.

We walk down Broad Street
then
up towards Jericho, dodging sightseers,
groups of students,
ambling,
laughing,
past the Ashmolean,
and I try not to remember that meeting
that I mistook for a date
and the way you looked at me
as if I had the capability,
the propensity and probably the desire,
to destroy anything in my way.

Lois and I walk
and I imagine us tied,
looped at the ankles,
two girls in a race,
stumbling, joined at the hip,
arms around each other's shoulders –
close, connected and charging
down a grassy strip of lawn,
chasing a vanishing sun.
Somehow I know
she needs me
and I need her.

Lois has short black hair
and eyeliner that makes her eyes seemed winged.
Her expression is difficult to fathom,
guarded, closed –
my own naked face
is too readable
and I am sick of being obvious,
easy to fool
easy to trick
easy to think you know my limits.

She walks quickly
and I rush beside her,
notice her cheeks are flushed
her eyes narrowed against the winter sun.

'Lois,' I say, clutching her coat,
'where are we actually going?
Do you know?'

She slows, as if after all she isn't sure,
and looks further up the road
perhaps deciding how far away
she wants to get before she feels safe.
I touch her sleeve, again.
'How about here?
Come on – let's get coffee, some food or something –
I'm starving.'

I cannot remember when I last ate.
Ari offered breakfast but
he was starting to disgust me,
lounging, half asleep,
replete on what he'd taken the night before,
this morning too.
My skin itches at the memory of what I let him do
to me.

Besides, Lois is too thin.
I like the idea of taking care of her
being the grown-up for once,
making her relax, maybe even laugh:
I don't mind if she laughs at me.

She follows me into the cafe
that leans crooked into the wall.
The dark smell of coffee hits me,
reminding me of you.

Everywhere I look.

This city speaks your name
every wall
every road
every patch of sunlight
is a memory of us.

I shut my eyes
then open them on the afternoon,
falsely bright with the pretence of adult certainty.
'OK, let's order drinks and food,
do you want wine?'

Lois shakes her head, decisive –
probably doesn't drink
certainly not to excess;
she reaches into her bag
and pulls out a folder, a file of essays
and notes,
printed documents
that look almost official.
Lois lays them out on the table between us,
with a pen
and a selection of highlighters
in colours I hadn't imagined exist.
I don't think I've ever owned a highlighter in my life

and am unsure whether or not to be impressed –
daren't ask if she uses spreadsheets,
don't want to look as if I'm taking the piss
(my life might have been a whole lot better
if I'd learned to use Excel).
She orders a glass of tap water,
student debt no doubt at the forefront of her mind,
and I guess
that this girl of nineteen
is probably wiser than me,
more astute,
manages her life
with the impeccable sense
I have never had.

She doesn't need me to make her eat or drink
to take her under my wing –

she'd be stupid if she did.

I order wine and take a breath.
'So – did you want to talk to me?
Is there something specific?'

I nudge her into speech
and she clears her throat.
'Yeah, right, actually, there is.'
Her accent, like mine was,
and still can become,
is regional – perhaps Midlands,
somewhere not far from here
but far enough to make her
different.

In that way we are both a little dull –
copper,
coins in the forgotten lining of a pocket.

She has a small stud in the side of her nose,
it looks pretty
but her clothes are the sort that
define her as possibly skint,
or maybe as someone who doesn't care –
principled. I expect she buys second-hand
to save the planet
not just to save her cash.

I judged her too fast.
I judge everyone too fast,
I look at the surface
instead of the depth
so I don't see wolves
when they're wearing
their best black tie,
gold-leaf-studded
smiles.

'So, I wasn't sure what happened yesterday,
in our tutorial with Tom,'
Lois says,
'but it looked like you have a problem with him
and I sort of gathered you were saying
I'd better watch out?'

I nod, yes, and
she goes on, voice quiet and circumspect,
careful not to give too much away.

'Yeah, well – about that –
I wanted to ask,
what did you mean, exactly?
If you don't mind telling me, that is.'

She waits.
I have to decide exactly how much I want to say,
if I can trust her with my secrets.

Because for a long time
I've wondered if anyone will ever like me again,
if I am the kind of person who can make friends
and keep them.
But what else do I have to do?
I have nowhere to be.
The alcohol buzz sets the words
spilling as I drain my glass and begin.

She doesn't react to the story
of our getting together,
my prize
and
the falling in love,
you leaving the mother of your kids.

She listens to me tell her
about my work,
the book of poetry
I wrote
that published when I was so young
and the one I began writing
and destroyed because of you.
And, of course, the research
into my poet: Charlotte Mew.

I pause and speak more about that –
how it stopped
when I didn't have so far to go,
how I got stuck,
then when I wanted to get back to work
it had gone.
You had stolen
everything that I'd done.

She listens, still and quiet,
as I lean across the table
fierce with fury –

arms waving fists clenching
voice raving.
Every time I say it it's the same:

You've driven me mad.

Maybe love is boring
in comparison with this.

But she's cool,
leans back.
'Yeah, OK, wow.
That's full on.
But I have to say that I'm not that surprised.'

'Really? Why not?'

'So. My best mate –
she left college at the end of last year,
and it was down to him,
your Tom, he treated her like dirt.
She was struggling,
but she would have been all right
with a bit of understanding.
But Tom was having none of it.
Basically – it was because of him
she quit.

I mean, I could see it coming.
There was always, just, something off,
the way he talks to some of the girls –
not me, OK, I don't mean me –
but I thought it was weird.
I'm not saying he's a perv
or anything like that
but
I didn't like him
at all.

And Celine fell apart.
She was basically in bits . . .'

I know what she's talking about.
The girl who accused you of bullying
but who you insisted was quite mad.
You mocked her anxiety,
ridiculed her fears,
said that you were a pussycat
in comparison to some other tutors.

But I don't think I've heard her name before,
you never dignified her with that –
and why didn't I care enough?
Why didn't I ask?

Lois keeps talking.
'Yeah, so
he's literally the worst tutor I've had.
Mr blue Twitter tick –
do you know he actually told us about that?
Literally no one cares.'

I nod.

I ask what happened.
'I'm sorry, Lois, I ought to know,
but Tom never really wanted to
talk about her.
I mean, he mentioned it of course,
but only to insist
that he'd done his best.'

She looks at me
and I try not to squirm,
not to feel like I let Celine down
by just not giving enough of a damn.

'Right, so she was great, my mate –
a really good laugh
and dead clever, too,
but she just had this thing,
never thought she deserved to be here.
She reckoned it was all a massive mistake
that she ever got a place.
And he saw it, Tom did. He knew.'

Lois waves her hands,
her face sharp with feeling,
she points a finger at me.

'And when Tom took the piss,
when he laughed at her in tutorials
and picked her apart,
said her essays were crap –
well, she couldn't cope.
And he must have noticed,
must have seen the effect it had.
She actually told him.
I said to her – go and complain,
tell him how it feels,
but she said he didn't even look at her.

He said,
if you can't take the heat,
then I suggest you go elsewhere –
*this isn't kindergarten, you know.*
And when she told him about her mental health,
he said,
*Why are you telling me?*
*If you're fragile, get some help.*
*Or have you considered that perhaps*
*you're just not good enough?*

I was so angry
I nearly went to see him to complain

but she saw a counsellor
and talked to the Junior Dean.
It got, like, extreme –
she wouldn't eat, couldn't sleep.
He denied it,
she lost it,
she was so close to the edge.
And now she's left, gone home,
and I'm so bloody angry.
I could literally kill him.'

That poor girl.
I don't doubt it's true.
How many more have had the Tom Abbot treatment?
Was I a special edition,
a bloody box set of humiliation?

'But why would he do it, Lois?
It just doesn't make sense?'

'Some people get off on it.
I'd say he's a total narcissist.'

'But he wasn't always like that—'
I stop. I won't excuse you –
maybe you've always been bad.

I chose to interpret
your arrogance as another body part,
an essential organ you would be less without.

'Anyway,' Lois says,
'what you've been saying,
it just seems to fit,
'cos, look, right –
I was at this lecture the other week
and I knew I'd heard the reading
he was giving somewhere before

but he was definitely acting like it was his original work –
so when I went back to the library,
I looked it up in the journals online,
found the book,
the chapter –
and I made notes –
I photocopied it, just to be certain, you know.'

She extracts a sheaf of paper from one of her files,
pushes the pages under my nose.

'What I mean is
I believe you,
about what he's done.
It pisses me off, basically,
and
I don't see why he should get away with all this shit.
How dare he make my best mate fall apart
when he's winging it himself, just like everyone is?'


## CONFESSION

I tell Lois everything.
Again.
She wants to
make notes
and I watch her transcribing my story
in careful handwriting.

Lois has no interest in the narrative
of my heart
hung up like a Christmas stocking
and ignored.
She is not bothered about how sick and empty
I say I feel
or about the love I tell her was between us
once.

She wants the proof of what you've done.
She has a lawyer's eye,
wants hard evidence
and prefers anger to tears.
Tough love.

There is no time for wallowing, she says,
or for me to lose the plot.
Better to concentrate on
facts.
The terrible
blood and guts of revenge
can wait
to be attended to once we have
the situation clear.

She should be a judge,
guardian of justice and truth.
I like her style,
her smooth face
that doesn't betray a moment's doubt
in what I have to say.

Afterwards she asks,
'So, what's the plan?'
The look in her eyes is expectant.
I look back at her.
Shrug.
'I haven't got a bloody clue.'

'You're not going to let him get away with it, though?'

'Well, obviously, no –
but I think I blew it,
storming into his room,
carrying on.
He brought Margaret Browning in,
and she thought I was nuts.
Lois, I'm sorry – I think I screwed it up.'

'If he's passing off other people's work as his own
then the university needs to know.
If he's bullying people off the course,
if this book he's publishing is based on your work –
there's no way you can just let that pass.'

'Yeah well,
it's my word against his.
Why should anyone believe me?
No one believed Celine, did they?'

Lois looks unconvinced –
'No.
But come on.
You've got to do something
for all of us,
for Cece,
for all the others that he might hurt.
Where's your self-respect, Emma?
Or has he taken that, too?'

I still can't answer her,
still don't feel
that we have a chance against you
or that anyone will ever listen to me again.

They all think I'm mental –
even Ariel.

I stare at my hands, wish I could read the lines
on my palm, the pattern of my life,
the best way forward.
Clenching my fists, I close my eyes
and find girls with paper
pens
scissors
ink and fire
and slowly, catching so slowly,
the light of an idea strikes.

Lois reaches towards me,
easing out of the straight-backed
professionalism of our meeting.
'Yeah?' she says,
'Have you thought of something?'
My lips curve into
the smallest of smiles.
I touch her hand and say,
'OK, listen, so –
maybe we go about this by stealth.'


## RETREAT

'You're back.'
It's hardly a welcome,
but better than a fuck off.

You open the door
and here we are again –

how much of our relationship
has been played out in this hallway?
One of us always either
coming or going,
as if no one can decide if they want to stay.

'I thought you'd left.'
Do I detect hope
or despair
in your voice?

Is it
love
in your eyes,
or relief,
indifference or disgust?

I don't know if I trust myself
to interpret you –
but you let me step closer,
and I say,

'Well, yes.
I thought I had, too,
but
it seems I can't keep away.'

It seems I can still lie.
It seems I can cry,
and you accept that this is an apology,
and I wonder why I never
played up to this more,
why I acted like I was fine
when I was dying inside.
I should have shown you the colours and shapes
you wanted –
gifted you with the sounds required, let you taste my pain,
the salt on my face.
I should never have tried to be brave.

A man like you requires a more subtle approach –
an ambush that you can't anticipate.
But if I'd known how tears might work
in my favour
I might have used them as leverage before.

Why has it taken me so long to realize that
you like it when I'm weak?
How stupid of me
not to see
that beauty
and brains
and bodies
are currency –
the only way I can win this game
is to turn every single trick.

So I will learn the colour of acquiescence
and disguise transgression,
I will assume transparency and apologize
as many times as you need
for making a scene,
or embarrassing you.
I will say,
'Tom, please forgive me,'
in every language of the world.

I say it now, and
your exhalation
fills the room – walls shift, big
like a birthday balloon, buoyant with relief,
and you take my hand, hold me close, we dance on air,
in the evening gloom,
                              weightless,
                                        lifted and floating towards the ceiling.

The mirror above the fireplace catches us
and I barely recognize the look on my face.
The chiselled certainty of intent.
The steel in my eyes.

I am resolute

but oh, so pliant, too.

Static prickles and
I buzz with electricity,
the dread of discovery a tremble under my skin:
like a thief hiding beside you, I judder and jump,
sizzle and crackle with a fear
that erupts as a cough
and a laugh.
I hide my face, too bold,
and you wonder if I ought to see someone who might help
to solve the problem of my
self.

Arms, calves, buttocks, thighs tingle and leap
when you touch me.
I stand aside,
let you pass
and try to disguise the shiver of desire
to       trip       you       up.

You pour drinks,
for you – and me –
put on music
(Mozart, your go-to for moments of triumph)
and you pull me on to your knee and kiss me.

'Are you staying?' you ask later,
after we have been to bed.
Why do you seem to like touching me
so much more than you did?
Is it because you have lanced the threat?
Eased out the pus of my feelings
and filled the hole;
                        more of you and less of me?

You run your hands through my hair
and pile it on my head.
'You know. And here's a funny thing,
You always reminded me
of Lizzie Siddall
        – Rossetti's muse.
Do you remember? That exhibition?
I didn't say so then,
you seemed so young,
but your hair, your skin.
I wanted you so much that day –
did you guess?'

No.
I just remember the
humiliation.

The raw red itch on my neck
drawing blood when I scratched,
ripping holes with my nails.
And poor Lizzie –
the suffering archetype
who froze for hours,
gave up her own art to sit still for a man,
lost her baby and then,
depressed and afraid, overdosed.
The analogy is too close for comfort
but I don't point this out and
instead I say,

'Yes, maybe – but I was pretty shy,
remember? So in awe.
I know I wanted you
from the first day we met,
but I thought you barely saw me.
I tried to tell myself it was just a crush,
that I'd get over you.
I never thought you'd like me back.'

You laugh quietly,
stroke my cheek –
'Emma, I *love* you back, despite
all the havoc you've wreaked.
You know I never wanted you to leave me.'

'I'm sorry.'
I put it into words again,
give you more of what you want,
grovel and bow and scrape.
'I'll retract my accusations, if you like,
apologize to your students
and, of course, to Margaret.'

You stretch, take up the bed,
long legs

everywhere,
body strong, muscled, relaxed.
'Perhaps, but you do understand
that Margaret didn't really
take in a word you said –
darling, you weren't making sense –
no doubt she's worried about the state of your mental
    health
but, well, we can explain
how difficult things have been for you.
It won't count against you, Em – I'll make sure of that.'

I nod,
bury my face in your chest,
close my eyes
and bite my tongue,
scratch
at my arm
where the itch, the patch of skin, has grown
reptilian
in the crook of my elbow,
viciously dry.

You still my hand, hold my fingers in yours
too tightly,
guide my hand
down your body,

we start again
and this time
you have no idea what's in my head.

I wonder if you ever did.

## PLANS

I am working
like a woman possessed
and you say you are happy
that I haven't left.

I take my time to think and plan
as February shivers into life
omened with dead things,
a rat –
grey and hopeless in the gutter –
and the body of a half-formed frog
near the river, jawed at by a cat,
its entrails splayed and dry.
I read these signs and feel the air change.

You come home early
and pour strong drinks
and cook with butter, garlic, wine:
sauces dripping with cream and olive oil.
You feed me and
I wonder if I'm getting fat
as winter passes into spring.

But you say you like my curves
and tell me to wear the clothes
you like best,
dress me up in
underwear made of silk
that sticks up my arse,
driving me mad.
You want me to look pretty,
to grow my hair
so long you can wrap it around my neck
when we're in bed.
And when I almost choke you gasp,
'Fuck, Emma, yes.'
And I bare my teeth and bite your flesh.

I am swollen,
fruiting ideas.

I watch you swim in your sleep
your arms wheeling through air
as you grunt and gasp –
and I hold my pillow close to my chest
so I don't press it over your face.

Ari texts
every day.
I don't tell you how he bothers me
like a fly rattling a windowpane.

We meet so I can tell him
to leave me alone.

I tell Ariel I'm staying with you.
I try to feel sorry for him
but don't have it in me to care enough
about his predicament.
I mean, what exactly was it we had –
a one-night stand?
A fledgling friendship?
He has no right even to this sliver of time,
or the effort it takes to expel
these words.

He pours his tea,
slams the pot back on the table,
making it shake.
'But I thought you were angry –
he cheated, right?
I thought there was something there.
I thought we clicked.'

I sigh. He's a child.

'Everyone cheats, Ari,
in one way or another –
I've decided to let it go,
God, I'm no saint either.
There was what I did with you, for a start –
I never told Tom about that.'

Ari twitches, runs his hands through his hair –
guilty, maybe, nervous,
and scared of what you might think
of your star pupil's
dick
in your girlfriend's mouth
and her cunt on his lips,
and I know that it's foul,
all this
bad language, but these are the words
you like to use
when you screw me
and I smile because
you don't know the words I will use to undo you.

I smile at Ari and touch his hand.
'Look, I'm sorry if you're upset
but it's not going to happen again.'

'So, you used me?'

'No.
I did like you.'
I suppose that's true, but it's hardly the issue
right now,
although maybe it is
the issue; that is,
of his ego
and my audacity
in rejecting whatever he had which he thought
I needed.

'But – Ari, the thing is,
I've got a lot going on.'

He doesn't finish his tea,
leaves it still steaming
and weak with milk
on the table.
He leaves me,
shrugging into the afternoon.

I am happy that I can write myself free
with a gluttonous vocabulary that
feasts on revenge.

You can't please everyone all the time –
my mother's motto, wearily moaned
when my brother and I would fight,
and I've never given her credit for
the things she could have taught me.

Ariel can think what he wants,
deal on his own with his
resentment.

I make my way home – the first Tuesday in Lent –
and stop
at the church
find my way inside and sit at the back
staring at Our Lady
cradling her baby,
listening to the priest talk about
patient suffering and
how it will be rewarded.

Sod that.
I'm no Griselda.
I have nothing to prove.
I leave before Communion
and let my rage fly me home.

## SURGE

Time begins to pass as it won't in winter –
spring sun comes on
strong and
I watch the sprouting shoots of green in my garden
and get down to work.

I study hard,
am back on track with my research,
while another woman keeps the house clean
and a delivery man brings the food we need
so I can concentrate on what matters most.


## BIRTHDAY

The mirror returns your smile better than I can.
'Forty-one,' you say and I ignore the
invitation to offer congratulations and
if you were expecting a present, well,
think on.

Margaret comes for Sunday lunch
with a cluster of other friends
and I cook as you pour drinks.
We paint a picture of domesticity:
there is harmony in the way I measure,
stir, roast and fry, press my tongue into the salt
of secrecy, the spice of silence.

'Emma's doing so well,' you announce to the room;
you share that you're pleased I'm in therapy
and am working again.
'She's dealing with whatever it was that
made her break down so spectacularly
last term.'

Margaret nods and touches my arm:
soft in velvet and smiles,
she is kind but shrewd,
and asks me to show her around.

We go into the garden,
pulling in air.

She picks rosemary, rolls and rubs it in her fingers
and breathes in the smell, and
we disappear into
the buzz of bees on daisy, forget-me-not, Solomon's seal,
the humming in the trees as
insects inch through the long grass,
catch the flashing yellow of a brimstone butterfly and
worms writhing lurid pink,
jellied with potential.
We watch the earth coming alive,
the gathering of industrious things
whose instinct it is to persist,
to halve
themselves, begin again to grow, whatever the circumstances,
no matter the threat of beaks or claws.

Whatever sugar there is to suck
will be sucked,
whatever earth there is to turn
will be turned,
there will be nests built

and then abandoned.

Margaret asks me how I'm getting on:
'I won't press for details, but I will just say
that I know it can't be easy.'

She means *you*,
that she knows you can't be easy,

that you are another thing to water and tend
and watch.

I snap a daisy from its stem and hold it out.
'It's fine. All good.'
She takes it, pushes it behind her ear and nods
as you call us back inside.

The lunch is a success,
you praise the wine,
the sauce,
the cake I have made that rose triumphantly
and which I decorated with a steady hand,
writing your name, looking forward to the large
slice I'd take.

You have taught me all about service
and the murderousness
of appetite.

I wonder what I taste like now.

Your friends praise you
and toast your good health,
toast your new book,
your career,
your future
and us.

Later, in bed,
lying in the darkness
and holding hands,
you say you have forgiven me for everything,
for behaving as if I was unhinged,
but you warn me very carefully
that I was really very ill
and next time I get to that point,
the point where I feel that I might be losing

my grip,
I must tell you
fast
so you can help.

I seem to like the softness of your voice,
I seem to be so compliant.
Leaning towards you, I kiss your cheek
and say,
'Thank you, Tom,
for everything you've done.'

I convince you that I have convinced myself
that you took nothing, after all;
everything was there
where it should have been –
in other words
the empty files
were figments of my troubled mind.

I imagined the breach
of my privacy
and the fingerprints all over my keys.
I imagined the thesis so clearly typed.
I imagined how close I was to the end.

And, after all,
there was nothing to steal,
I'd just had some thoughts
that weren't terribly original.
In fact –

'We collaborated, Emma,
you should be pleased
that it's worked out so well.
I think together we've taken this work further
than you might have done alone
and I'm sure this experience will stand you in good stead.'

I smile and nod
and tell you how clever you are.


## WORK

You deliver me to the library and leave me to it
whilst you disappear into a lecture theatre
and say you'll see me later at home.

I sit and read a bit,
stare out of the window,
distracted, listening to the students' laughter.
Late, or lazy, they chatter,
oblivious to the precariousness of self.

I think of how
you think you own my words,
that I owe you this work
and this book I'm creating
and the years of my dreams held in its pages.

My fingerprints dissolve as I write
and perform the labour you can't be arsed to undertake.

My wrists are thicker,
my fingers swell
and what was soft is hardening
and calloused with intent.

I'm angry enough to want to see you
beg
on your knees,
crucified in public,
reputation shredded,

finally castrated.

I cannot not plot. Will not
sit silent,
allow you credit you haven't earned,
let you parse me
parcel me
lock me up like Colette,
counting my words
behind those gates.

What you don't know is
I am working my way into the metal –
I am iron,
hard as nails,
and, heated, I can take on shapes,
bend myself, twisting, becoming the lock
impenetrable so your key no longer fits:
however you work it
inside me

I will
shut you out.

But for now I do my time.

～

It's evening when I cycle home.

You have bought me a bike,
shiny red with a basket on the front,
and I breathe in the May evening.
Early summer, full of shadows
and the murderous sweetness of magnolia trees
spilling white petals all over the road,
dangerous in their slippery selves,
waiting to trip me if
I do not go carefully –

Lois tells me all the time to
*Watch out,*
as if there are ghosts
or spies in the pipes of the house or
pushing up between the paving stones.

The roses I planted have not yet bloomed,
although I water them daily,
watch them and wait for flowering.

I stand outside
breathing hard, breathless from the ride,
bicycle by my side,
and stare at the path
strewn with vines: morning glory
torn up by the roots and discarded like trash.
I presume we've been visited by some poltergeist.

'Tom,' I call, opening the door,
panting your name.
'Have you seen this?'

You stand on the step in bare feet and shrug.
'I was trying to help.
It's just a weed,
right?'

(We don't see the world the same way –
you don't find beauty in the mundane.
Even a weed should have its day.)

The garden grows despite you;
to spite you
I planted things to make you sneeze
and you blow your nose,
and retreat.

Trying to bridge the gap
between our perceptions of the world,

keeping everything smooth, for now –
I don't tell you you're a twat,
but bend and bury the roots back into the crumbling soil
and hope for the best.

When I come into the house,
last sun in my eyes,
I hallucinate bodies
pocked with glowing contusions
the dusty air gaping with holes.

# TRINITY TERM

## UNDERCOVER

You begin again
back in college
third term tutorials and students
panicking about their finals.

I paint my nails and watch you pack your bag
while you complain of the smell
and I wonder when you will guess
that I am planting poison.

The train to London is noisy
the sun a yellow scab
hot enough to make the city stink.
I walk fast, away from the tube and the crowds,
to a library where it is quiet and cool.

A change of scene
is sometimes all you need
to do something amazing.

Lois meets me in the stacks
and we whisper,
heads close,
strands of hair
mingling –
you wouldn't know if I was her
or she were me –
I like this blurring,
co-conspirators
conjoined in our machinations.

'OK?' she asks.
Her breath is sweet, like Coca-Cola,
her eyes shadowed, tired.
I know she will have stayed up reading for hours:
she is determined to help.

'I'm fine.'

'And him? Tom?'
The way she says his name always makes me shiver –
and if loathing had a colour
it would be the yellowing pallor
of Lois's cheeks.

'Oh God, he's on top form.
He's got a slot on *In Our Time* this week,
so, you know,
we're awfully jolly right now
and also
the book tour's being planned,
they've bought the rights in the US and want him to
do the universities, East Coast and West.
Tom's like a pig, Lo,
wallowing in the stink of his own shit.'

She pulls a face,
and I read her immediately –
that she thinks you're disgusting,
is amazed I can bear
to share your bed
and accept your breath and sweat and skin;
a Sadeian woman fed sweets
to make her stomach gripe.

We have our own
language brimming with spite, vengeful
but justified.
Born out of gaps,

our attack will be almost invisible,
virtually incomprehensible:
we know new ways to express
what's hiding underneath,
can
peel up skin and find where the
wickedness waits.
We will explode from there like arterial blood:
detonating mines –
ripping flesh.

We like playing with
meanings that could exist but don't –
semantic lacunae, I joke.
It all feels so
terribly scholarly
in the funniest way –
and somehow easier to cope when I go home
to offer up my pretence of love.
It makes me laugh that I
know so many things that you don't.

Give me the confidence of a mediocre white man
who thinks he has the right to
a woman's work –
her words
and womb
and everything else.

We handle books as if they are dirty bombs
with the power
to shred you,
render you impotent
and unemployable.

And if it's cruel to set this trap
I don't care.

I show Lois the poem I wrote last night
and she holds it against her chest
right by her heart
and nods,
*Yes*.


## ARIEL, AGAIN

'What are you doing here?'
I confront him and
he flushes,
embarrassed to be found
watching us.

'Were you spying on me?' I ask.
He stares at the paperwork
the books in my pile
and assesses the words written on my screen.
I slam it shut.

He's just another man
with no idea of boundaries.

'What are you doing here?' he wants to know,
as if he has the right to information
about my life and whereabouts.
The librarian shushes us,
and a man with a Tupperware box
full of lunch
sighs.

Lois stares at Ariel with furious eyes
and I introduce them whilst I pack things into my bag.
Ari follows us to the exit,
Lois bats at him as if he were a fly,
trying to get him to move out of her way.

He won't take the hint,
sits near us on the train
trying to talk to me,
texting me
when I ignore him
over and over again.


## PILGRIMAGE

Another hot day and a tube spits us out in Bloomsbury
to wander the streets where Charlotte would have walked
as a girl, to school and home.
Doughty Street,
Mecklenburgh Square.

I keep looking, as if I might find her here,
but I'm too late, over a hundred years
between her
and me.
Does anyone else stop to wonder

outside the unlucky house, stare at a belated blue plaque
or read the other signs

she left behind?


## NEWSNIGHT

You sit in make-up
and I watch you
watching yourself in the mirror,
rehearsing what you plan to say –
your lips twitch over the lines,
everything pre-planned,
even smiles, gestures of agreement
or grimaces, wry and intellectual.

Education –
and the university's commitment to diversity,
the joy of state-school talent
(yet more exhausting irony),
how you're sharing the space
to include those who might have previously been
overlooked.

You sit round the table
opposite a Minister for Culture,
another for Sport,
and bandy opinions;
you talk
over a woman to your right –
the host –
and almost roll your eyes
when a fellow lecturer –
who just so happens to be a young
black woman –
cuts in
and I wince

but then,
when you are kissed in the green room,
and those government saps tell you
how brilliant you are,

I wonder how long this has been going on
and how you get away with it.


## VACATION

You trust me to make a plan
to take your daughters on holiday
for a week.

I decide camping will be nice,
used to love the Brownie Guides
and the campfire evenings
smoky with the magic of being outside at twilight.
We'll give them a taste of good fresh air
and you will get to know them.

Hours trapped on the M5,
you stare through the windscreen,
pretend you can't hear Tabitha whine and
turn up Radio 4,
until you give in and we stop
for another wee.

I buy ice cream.

Your face is sour, but I remind you,
'It's a holiday,' and laugh at your frown,
laugh again
when the car is covered in crumbs and rubbish
and the children fall asleep
smeared in sweetness.

We are holidaying not so far from your mother's place.
I haven't mentioned it
and don't plan to go if I can help it
but the look on your face
as we pass the turn-off
tells me it's on your mind –
that you haven't seen her since Christmas, that
she hasn't seen the children –
and I wish I had it in me to be kind
but I can't feel sorry for her,
her loneliness is too sour.

You are not adept at tents
in the same way that you are inadequate at
tasks like painting window ledges

or mending punctures,
fixing boilers.
It's a good job you can pay a plumber and
a painter
and I can mend
my own mind.

Somehow we manage to pitch before it rains
and find a place that sells fish and chips,
sit in a shelter by a manmade lake.
'It's not Amalfi, Emma, right?'
you complain.

(I remember, then,
how I missed the sunset,
the spectacle of light
becoming night,
in bed early,
my head splitting with too much wine.

I told you I would get up to see the sun rise.

You rolled your eyes,
doubting me,
underestimating my ability to be out of bed,
underestimating
what I notice and know
about the world.)

A small dog barks at us
and Martha feeds the ducks,
splashes and squeals in small puddles,
while Tabitha tells you in a serious voice
about Charles II – very fortunate
to have had such a sensible nephew in
William of Orange –
and quite taken by this line of chat
you talk about Dryden,

Milton,
the Glorious Revolution,
while she yawns in your lap
and I remember that you were –
you are –
you could be –
a brilliant man.

'Please come.'
The coincidence of your mother
on the telephone
and the news of your father's imminent demise
break the spell
and we're in the car again
before I get the chance to stay behind.

She is waiting for you,
wants to take the children to her
dying husband's bedside.
I shake my head and you nod and
put your arm around your mother to hold her up,
exhausted from the drive – but, for once,
I see something in you that I admire.

I've never seen you cry.

But later
in the grey dawn
grief twists your face
into a new shape.

Hannah comes to take the children back home,
extricate them from Annette's smothering
and their father's impatience,
his distracted rages
as his mother complains
that he's sending them away too soon.

And the holiday that barely began
is done.

We stand by Hannah's smart new car
and she asks me how I am.
I can smell her perfume –
oranges, like Seville, and the intoxicating idea
of being free of you.
I breathe her in,
so tanned and smooth,
uncreased by any of this.

I unrumple my skirt, smooth out my hair, regret
the library tinge to my skin and say,
'Oh, fine, I'm keeping out of their way,
letting them get on with it.
I'd rather be leaving with you,
to be honest.'

She shrugs.

'So do. There's room in the car,
I can drop you back.'

The temptation of leather seats,
air conditioning
and Hannah's conversation.

Gravel twists beneath my shoe
and here you are
as I'm about to throw myself into her car
and escape.
You put an arm around my shoulder,
lean in to kiss your girls goodbye,
eyes leaking,
grief speaking for you,
and I stay
again.

# LATE AUGUST

At home
I sit beside you and follow your finger.
I want to be outside sitting in what is left of the sun
on my patch of lawn
amongst the overgrown grass and riot of wild flowers.
The seeds I threw
in spring have grown –
centaury, musk mallow, wild marjoram.

I could be walking by the river,
and diving deep to swim
amongst the fish and reeds, emerging clean.

But we are inside,
in the muggy heat of this small room,
my thighs
are glued to yours,
we are gummed together, sticky with sweat.
You trace under the words
and we read
as if I am only just learning how to decipher
the sounds,
blend them, lisping, like a child.

'Look,' you say,
the manuscript between us –
you have printed it off
one last time
so that we can check it
carefully.

My job is to ensure the footnotes are correct,
the references,
to do the grunt work,
hours of eye-strain
and headaches

on your behalf;
but first you lead me
chapter by chapter as
we admire the scope and depth
of the introduction, and the development of
my original idea
as the chapters progress.
You compliment me on the hard work I have done
to ready the manuscript for publication,
flick through the final chapters,
and read aloud the occasional verse as
we discuss how helpful it is
for young academics to be steered
by experienced hands.

'Emma, you've done well.
I don't praise lightly, as you know.
So I thought I might
include you in the dedication.'

I manage a smile and fake gratitude
for the kind thought,
then say,
'No, no need.
I would actually prefer not.'

It's all I can do not to kick you in the balls and run
as the finger that found its way
along those pages
works its way into my clothes,
fumbling buttons,
finding skin.

I have to do this too?
It's not easy
to go to bed with you,
a cage where I pretend to love you,
where I fake everything, fake truth –

but at least I'm writing
and making poetry out of this dead end.


## HEX

We play our games of poetry late into the night.
The moon observes, a milk stain on the carpet, smelling of
    the future.

I surprise you with words,
write the sickly disease
into your palm.

You ask me to repeat the verse, confused,
anticipating romance, devotion;
instead I take my nail and graffiti you with Shakespeare's
    curses,

that though I have sworn thee fair and thought thee bright
you are as black as hell
and dark as night.

I lick the appalling message on to your thighs
and slug trails of saliva, semen, sex
spill over the bed

and still you don't get it.

# MICHAELMAS TERM (2)

## LAUNCH

October,
a new slew of students to impress.
I go to the library
and then meet you for lunch.

Now you like to keep me close.
If I were on the loose, you think, it might
provoke another mishap, another lapse
in my sanity.
You care too much to run the risk.

Your colleagues talk about their work
and occasionally ask me
what it is I'm doing now,
perplexed by the very question.
Mostly they don't understand why I'm
still here.

It was part of our deal:
that I'd finish up the work on Mew
then begin something new.

The conversation went like this:
'I think she took too much of you,
sometimes immersion in a subject
can affect you like that
and the consequences
weren't pretty, were they, Em?

Perhaps a man this time –
male authorship
is so much more

defined,
structured by a sense
of certainty even whilst offering much scope
for the heart.
Play it a little safer –
who knows where this could go.'


You decided that William Cowper would be right for me,
focusing on his Miltonic filiation.
I thought it sounded shit
but nodded and promised to begin
thinking.
You didn't see me roll my eyes.


This fresh approach, as you call it,
could cost another four years of my life,
four years before I pass through the gates,
which means I'm almost back
where I began
with no record of that time;
I might as well not have been alive.


I'm as easy to wipe clean as a table after lunch.


And the first Thursday of the month is
publication day.


You wake early
and we breakfast on champagne.
I prepare the tray, bring it up to bed,
pop the cork and watch you gulp down a glass
in the grey shudder of the dawn.


I can feel your nerves begin to fry
with the bacon as you answer emails
and wait for congratulations.

The kitchen fills with smoke and I open the back door
and let in the wind as you rip into a slice of toast.

Your mother is the first on the phone
to tell you her copy has arrived –
she wants to know why you have written about
such a ghastly subject
as suicide and the poetics of death.

What was it that inspired your interest in such grizzly
    things?

I listen to you try to defend your themes
and laugh.
The morning ticks on.
You speak to your publisher,
agent,
publicist,
people,
and it's such a hot topic
that you need to whip up one thousand words
for the *Telegraph*.
I understand I am required again.

We go to your study.
I stand behind you
and steady your nerves,
hand on your shoulder,
feeling the undercurrents as your muscles tense
and I run a finger down your back.

I dictate
and you type –
we do it together, easy oiled machine,
I slip into gear, then you press send and
smile.

Squeezing my hand,
you tell me,
'Thanks,
just nerves, I think.
But I value your help, Emma,
it's good to have you here.'

We hug.
But I don't like the way you smell
any more.

On Sunday
I bring you the papers in bed
and together we enjoy the double-page spread –
the picture of you looking moody,
eyes sharp
behind the glasses,
and the text extolling your body of work.

*This latest book*
*establishes Tom Abbot's reputation*
*as one of our leading literary minds –*
(you boast of your success:
double first from Cambridge and
the rack of exams
on which your intellect was stretched;
your popularity and publications,
proof of your relevance) –
*Abbot charts new territory in*
*this masterpiece*
*and writes with such*
*tenderness,*
*such phenomenal rigour,*
*that one cannot help but be seduced*
*by this remarkably modern figure.*

I can hear Charlotte exclaiming from her grave,
my poet's head butting rotten wood,

fists raised in fury
as I read aloud of your
*heroic examination of Mew's lost verse*
*and commitment to challenging canonical*
*assumptions about the worth*
*of this woman's work.*

It is something of a literary coup
to have discovered after almost a century
what was firmly believed lost to dust:
Charlotte's late last poems
written before her demise –

her final message
into which you have breathed life;
an extraordinary insight into what drives us
into the arms of patient, painful death.

You deconstruct her methods:
read what was unsaid
and rip her wide open,
my transcendent
*red dead thing*,
to place her broken and bleeding
on the slab of your fame.


**PARTY**

More champagne.
I'm starting to feel sick when I smell it
and put down my glass
fingers sticky with the residue of celebration.

Lois moves close,
we whisper and
she asks me,
'This is killing me. When?'

'Not yet,' I tell her.
'Give it time.'

I am going to let you enjoy this for a little longer,
let you feel the rope,
let you run it through your fingers
as I'm tying you up.

Ariel joins us,
ignoring Lois,
and asks me where I've been,
why haven't I even said hello?

I kiss him and tell him how sorry I am,
how I've missed him, of course –
'Just busy with this crazy thing called life' –
my laughter as false as his leading smile.

Inserting himself between me and my friend,
he seems determined
not to let 'us' rest,
he hasn't forgotten those two nights in his bed,
although I've ignored his calls for months;
he is still petulant.
'You really stayed with him, then?'

'I had no choice,' I say softly,
trying to smile.
'He made it hard for me to leave –
and I suppose I must have wanted to stay.
Maybe I love him.
Look, I'm sorry, Ari.
Forgive me? Please?'

Picking up my glass again
I swallow the warm alcohol
and Ariel nods, drinks,
takes my hand and says,

'For sure. That's cool.'
We clink glasses and I let him
believe what he wants about what could be.


How I am interpreted
is up to them.
Let them make their assumptions.


'So what is it you've been doing?
You and the weird girl with the black hair?
When I saw you in the British Library, remember?
You were acting so strangely, like
you had something to hide.'


What if he knows?
What if we're discovered?
Wild stinging nettles prickle along my thighs,
inside my pants
running like hands up inside my stomach
spiking fear in my throat.
I cough, put down the glass before I spill everything.


Ariel looks at me
and something in his face tells me
that he too thinks that I am made of wax,
that he could be the one to melt me
and then scoop me up and palm me smooth and quiet.


Well, if that's the case, I wonder
what shape I'll take on next,
if he understands the power of
metamorphosis.


Speeches –
you stand
in the crowded room,
I spot your children at the front

holding Hannah's hands
and see how they look up at you,
to you,
despite everything.

Ari's hand is on my waist.

It's a shame that those little girls
will see the image of their father burst,
have to realize too soon that he
is as base as any of us,
but maybe they already see through you,
have wisely accepted that
disappointment starts early.

Twisting out of Ari's reach
I catch Hannah on her way out.
'Hi, how are you?'
She's been away with work
and took the girls along
so we haven't seen them in some time.
'Emma! You look well,
how lovely to see you
and – how wonderful –
Tom finished his book, thank God!'
There is an archness to her smile
and I blush,
look down,
nod yes
and mumble how happy I am.
'You must be relieved –
God, he was foul there for a while.
He's a new man tonight.
I wonder—'

She lets her words hang
but I say nothing, just look at her,
and she shrugs,

and tells me to
enjoy it while it lasts.

As we say goodbye
I let myself imagine for a moment
what she'll think
of the truth
and regret that we will probably never be friends.


## EXPOSED

The TV interview will be live –
it's a coup to be invited on to this show:
since when were academics
anyone's mid-morning go-to?
Since when did anyone give a shit
about Charlotte Mew?

But your agent knows the producer
and the topic's hot:
you can talk about mental health and suicide
and women silenced, the insult of being called
a *poetess* by Virginia Woolf, no less.
It's a bonus that you look so good.

'If you were old and ugly,'
she said, only half joking,
'it would have been a no.'

How we laughed at that.
How I cursed under my breath.

You didn't sleep last night and I sat up with you
and we talked and I answered your questions
as well as I could.

You thanked me
and kissed my hand, held my palm to your cheek –
'You know, I do know how lucky I am.'

I nearly told you then,
I nearly confessed –
but I didn't.

Honesty will have to wait its turn.

So this morning I answer the front door
and Lois strides inside, through the hall,
sits down at the kitchen table,
snaps my laptop open and finds the channel.

She raises her mug in a toast:
'Happy National Poetry Day, mate,' she laughs.

Hands shaking, I sit and sip – spilling
hot tea,
clumsily mopping it up
and spilling again.
I bang the table with my thigh
as I walk to the bin and feel
the instant bruise of it.
But Lois is calm.

'God, Em – please –
would you just
chill out.'

The theme tune.
Then the grinning presenters
on a bright green sofa,
the woman introduces you, Tom –
and for a moment
I want it to stop,
I can't bear to witness

what I know is about to commence –
and reach to slam the laptop shut –

Lois holds my fingers
tight in hers,
'Don't,' she says.
'It's time. You don't want to miss it, do you?
This is it, Em – everything we worked for.
Sit down.
Enjoy.'

The rash on my wrists and fingers flares
and I sit raking at the skin,
burning my mouth on my drink and swearing.

Why didn't you guess what it was I was up to?
Why haven't you seen through me
as I have seen through you?

The interviewer praises her guests
and introduces the great
Tom Abbot – the nation's favourite
Oxford don,
who's made poetry popular again,
and whose new work is unmissable,
extraordinary, unforgettable –
and honestly couldn't be more timely.

The guests on his sofa concur.

Lois rolls her eyes.
'Will she ever just shut up?
Looks like Tom's cast his spell there,
what an arse-licking load of crap.'

But it's true, you look good on screen;
at a distance
you look like the kind of man I'd like to meet.

We move on to the esteemed Amelie O'Rourke,
who's beside you on the sofa, maintaining her distance.
Joyce scholar,
Irish professor,
here to discuss the necessity of poetry in the modern world
as more than comfort,
but as a means of reaching out and connecting,
and, of course, Tom's new book:
a re-examination of the little-known
and vastly underrated genius
Charlotte Mew.

The discussion begins amicably
but I can't hear it above
the sizzle of my nerves
and the froth of blood too loud –
the wild heat of my horror
a fire in my ears.

'Tom, can you explain what it was
that first drew you to this enigmatic figure?
She was quite something else.'

You smile, lean forward, look into the camera,
speak with such genuine passion
that I almost believe you,

almost believe that you love her
as she deserves to be loved.

'It's her originality, the work sings
with extraordinary vigour and the power of her vision.
She was a truly inspirational creator.
But be honest, Christine, had you even heard of her?'

The host performs
a pantomime of sorrow at her ignorance
as you parrot words I said first

years ago, when I began –
my ideas then only a seed,
a speck of dust, a grain of sand.

But you could see the world there,
and I should have seen you
sooner, understood what I read
in your face
when you looked at me when we lay in bed.

You saw an opportunity,
a chance, fresh lands to exploit,
a pirate let loose on the high seas of my hope.

You speak with confidence and charm,
reaching out with the slow seduction of your laugh,
arms spread wide across the sofa;
your chest,
your thighs,
all that power.
I can see the bored housewives
swooning as they do their ironing,
the Amazon chart quickly rising.

You tell of Hardy, Sassoon, so many great names
and how they lauded Charlotte
until she slipped into obscurity
and, again, the tragedy of this.

I groan. Swear. Beg to turn it off but
Lois tells me to *shhhh* and
the conversation turns
to the poems Mew wrote before her life
ended, too soon –
the work she'd produced just before she died.

And you begin to pontificate,
leaning forward and hogging the camera,

expounding on my thesis
about the work of suicidal minds and
the sensuality of skeletons buried alive;
the tragic passion of women
for whom love was *murdered joy,*
to quote Mew herself, speaking of Emily Brontë,
her poems are *the love songs
of a woman who never loved.*

What loss that she lost herself to
the grave seduction of death.

You call on Plath, Anne Sexton,
and recite verbatim from one of Mew's
newly discovered works.

The lanky lines and childlike rhymes are all hers –
and mine.

The genius
of our verse combined.

We speak – the waves of air
astonished at our nerve.

I run to the sink, run the tap
and put my face into the stream of water,
drowning my disgust.

I shouldn't have dragged poor Charlotte
into this.
She didn't deserve to become a hoax.

Dripping wet, I bite my knuckles,
screw my eyes closed,
but it's too late to stop;

I've used my poet to humiliate
the man I hate. The man I loved.

Lois pulls me back.
I have to watch.
You tell the viewers of your excitement in
discovering something so long believed destroyed:
the last writing
of one of our greatest neglected female voices,
a poet who should be on every university syllabus;
really – you pause for dramatic effect – she is truly
    glorious.

Lost for a century,
the story goes that she used her last poems
as roll-ups, and smoked her genius to death.

There's laughter – you join in –
you tell them of her mother's parrot, Wek, who hated men,
and the umbrella which she carried like a weapon –
of course she was only tiny,
this ungainly 'imp with brains' –
you indulge yourself and us with bits of trivia
that prove just how crazy Charlotte was
and gosh you're glad to have this chance to share her
story and this new work with us.

The interviewer laughs, and smiles, murmurs her respect,
and you are congratulated once again.

Lois watches me, wide-eyed.
And I am speechless, too, ashamed
of the memory
of Lois and I trawling through archives
finding clues
and piecing together fragments from letters and stories
to create verses
out of nothing,

to write lines
with a ghostly pen
then hand them over to you –
watching as you read,
dreading discovery,
pulse fading, plummeting:
what would you do to me if you found out?

Tom, you fool,
you didn't even notice
one of the poems from my prize-winning collection.
I made it so easy for you.

(If only you'd read me
as I deserve to be read.)

Professor Amelie breaks in,
pleasantly professional,
and speaks slowly, seriously,
her gravitas undermining your exclamations.
She wants to know –
though whilst it's interesting
to hear this work, it's certainly roaring with emotion –
how thorough you have been?
If you're sure
of the authenticity
of the poems you are citing?

Here we go.

We weren't sure
if Amelie would come through –
we sent her a proof of your book
and a letter
that explained its flaws,
and wondered if she might not want to destroy you on air.
Perhaps it was Celine's note
that convinced her in the end.

You sputter and tell her of course
you are.

Then Professor O'Rourke
proceeds to deliver
a series of blows
proving beyond a shadow of a doubt
that Mew wrote nothing of the sort.

'I'm afraid you've mistaken
your sources, Tom,
or else this is some kind of dreadful hoax.'

'Perhaps you're just not aware . . .'
The professor is afraid that this so-called discovery
is something of a joke
amongst those who know
a hell of a lot more about this poet
and have spent years ensuring that she is
not quite as misunderstood
as he thought.

'What do you mean?' Tom asks.

Amelie remains pleasant,
wondering how he could have believed
he'd get away with a mistake of quite this magnitude.

'This work is just not Charlotte Mew's.
The voice – as you say – whilst startling
is unambiguously not her own.'

The professor explains that my poet
never wrote about her own death,
nor dying,
in quite these sorts of tones.
If anything she was far more impersonal,
although the tragedy of humanity was of course her theme;

these words are unequivocally –
quite obviously –
not
hers.

'Where on earth did you find this material, Tom?
I mean, in many ways it's parodical –
surely you knew?'

There is silence,
just breathing –

you stutter something about the Bodleian
your wider reading
access to the estate
and visits to Bloomsbury you never made.

Amelie makes it clear, in case you haven't quite heard:
'Tom, these poems are not the real thing.
I'm amazed someone didn't notice.
Frankly, it's utterly astonishing.'

She smiles –
in pity, or triumph?

The presenter looks intrigued.
'Well – this is exciting –
are you saying that our Oxford scholar
has made a mistake?'

Tom is green, then red,
then grey,
trying to find a way to disappear or just
to talk his way clear, but there's no time,
no chance for him to equivocate his way out of this,
the segment finishes and he stands
and strides off camera,
swearing loudly just off screen

as the presenter stutters apologies and
someone somewhere laughs.

Twitter explodes:
#BOOM!
#hoistbyhisownpetard
#whatashambles
#TomAbbotisanarse
#whoonearthwasthatstupidman
#whatanembarrassment
#mansplainedhimselfoutofajob
#Oxbridgenob

*THANK YOU,*
I text Amelie O'Rourke.

When I heard she'd be his fellow guest
I thought it only right
to raise a couple of questions.

And she – being thorough,
working in the interrogative mode –
took me –
a fellow academic –
at her word.

I told her I was your student,
not your lover,
I told her I was concerned that you
were not really as clever
as you thought.
Well – I said that in so many words.

It seems as though she agreed.

## PUTTING THE BOOT IN

Lois hands me my phone
and I make the call –
the journalist at the *Guardian*
who said she'd be keen to talk
as soon as I was ready.

We have given her sources:
me,
Celine,
I even mentioned Hannah,
although I doubt she'll get involved.

Either way we have enough
to destroy you, Tom,
in one of those Sunday supplements
of which you're so fond.

Maybe it's too much –
perhaps I'm
twisting the knife
but I feel the need to finalize this.
Whatever – I'm sure you'll tell your side of things,
I'm sure you'll find
someone to represent your
story.


## RECKONING

My bag is packed again.
I have a passport
and a ticket that you have paid for
and I am leaving
just as soon as I can,
just as soon as I have said goodbye.

I wait for you to come home.
To run would be cowardice
and I think I ought to see the aftermath and explain.

It was a shame
you thought that to make yourself big
I had to be small
so I suppose I wanted to make you crawl
like an ant
under my shoe
and with my steel heel
eviscerate you.

Should I have murdered you
a year ago?
Lugged your corpse into the garden and
buried you outside?
You'd have made a rich fertilizer and
I could have pretended I had no idea
where you'd gone –
I can dissemble with the best of them.
I could have laid a patio,
and inscribed a bench with your name
and a line of poetry
or two.

## UNRAVELLING

The front door opens,
slams back against the wall
and I ricochet to my feet.

You call. I respond.
And you follow my voice upstairs
to our bedroom

where I stand in a patch of sun
wondering:
will you be different now?

Your smart boots menace, heavy-footed,
slapping, creaking – a leather strike
as you climb towards me –

then push open the door
stand on the threshold, your shirt sticking to your skin,
forehead glistening.

It would be a lie to say that I am calm.
A lie to claim that my breath isn't as ragged
as yours. How stupid to want this denouement.

You can't look at me,
just ask the air,
'Was it you, Emma?'

I nod.
Stare at the dark patches under your arms.

'You wrote those poems?
Lied like that?
I can't believe that you would.'

'I did.'

What happened to screaming?
To swearing and hating?

'But why?'

I almost laugh.
I should have anticipated that question
should have had my answer ready.

'If you don't know, then
I'm afraid
I don't know what to say.'

The restraint of it. The politeness.
I wish I wasn't crying.

I wish you weren't either
but our bodies are our own betrayal.

Did you cry in the studio?
All the way home?
Do you know what it feels like now?

Your hands hang useless by your sides,
hands that have touched me everywhere
and will never touch me again.

I used to want your mark on me;
the flourish of your pen, dripping ink, indelible
beneath my skin.
The artist's name in the corner of their work.

You clench a fist and explain your distress,
emptying your pockets of humiliation,
loose change that clatters to the floor and rolls against the
    walls.

'How could you?
My college, my students,
my mother, for God's sake –
I'm a laughing stock,
Emma, my agent's going mad.
The bloody publisher's enraged.
Fuck – I don't understand why you'd do this
after everything
I've done for us.'

I shake my head.

'You've been lying to me all these months?'

'Yes.
I wanted to hurt you. You took my work.'

'Revenge? Seriously? You petty bitch.'

'Petty?'
We stare at each other through the tears
and I look at the room,
the bed I made this morning with clean sheets,
plumping pillows,
smoothing carefully, corners neat –
leaving all in order.
Was that supposed to be
some sort of recompense for this?
Thinking that at least you'd have the comfort of the fresh air
on linen, might smell the love that I put in
to small things. Not all was driven
by my hate.

Because this time I will not be here
to smooth balm, apply unguents,
            spread        my        legs.

I think of
all the rooms in all the buildings,
the beds where we have woken together,
and how we have slipped
so out of time
that you have not heard my heart beat in years.

'I'm going now' – I check the time on my phone –
'don't want to miss my train,
and there's no point me hanging around here,
not now it's all over.

I guess you'll blame me, hate me
for a bit; for ever.
Whatever.
That's up to you. It doesn't matter.
But I thought you'd realize what I'd done.
For God's sake, Tom, why didn't you?'

You stare at me, still slack with shock.

This should feel better, should be easier
than it is.
We are all tears and sighs and guilty sweat.

I suppose I am to blame, in part:
I told you I'd discovered Charlotte's lost verse –
the poems people hoped still existed
but which do not.

Oh, Charlotte – what has been lost?
What didn't we read
because you didn't think it was good enough?

Or perhaps my poet only teased when she said
the paper she rolled and filled with tobacco
was a manuscript –
maybe she just wanted to make them gasp
to make people believe she set her genius on fire.

But perhaps she just ran out of words,
ran out of hope that anyone would take
any notice.

You don't care about any of that,
rub the tears from your cheeks and drop on to the bed,
look up at me and reach out a hand,

'Emma, come on.
Help me out here;
you can't do this and then just fucking go.'

Of course you're not going to admit
that you're the fool.

You won't concede
but begin to rally excuses
panic building defences out of bad air.

I won't collude or acquiesce,
won't touch you and start all that again.

I straighten the pillow,
detach myself,
pick up my things
and walk away,
bang my bag
down the stairs,
through the hall.

I don't look back.

Don't hear my name on your lips,
or you yelling that this isn't right,
don't hear
all the ways you're sure we can justify
the misunderstanding,
take back
the story and adjust its ending.

I don't hear you tell me that
I can fix this for you, I must fix this for you;
I owe you.

I close the front door
softly
and
go.

# HUMAN REMAINS

You have failed to bury me
deep in the footnotes,
nor squeezed me into the well
of your fountain pen.
I have slipped out from under the butter dish,

the human remains wholly here.

And in my bag there is more than clothes.

There is the book
I've written – it is everything I know.

Someone has promised to pay me
and maybe one day I'll pay you back
or
perhaps the scales have balanced now.

What was it the old Victorian said?
That of all the sorrows of womanhood
there is none more affecting than that of an Authoress.

What a hoot.
What did he know?

The roses are truly over.
Dropped petals write our epitaph
on to the scrub of grass, the leaves
littering the lawn.

The walk is slow.
I don't want to
leave this city behind,
the one that made me
and betrayed me,
stole so much of my heart –

but I guess I'm breaking up with these spires,
pulling them out from under my skin
like splinters or needles,
one by one.

The London train waits,
crowded, hot and impatient, full of people,
and I'm glad of the stench of their easy bad temper,
close my eyes and breathe in real life.

I sip from the can of gin and tonic,
feel the fizz up my nose,
celebratory, almost, text Lois that it's done,
I'm gone,
and dare myself to
look out of the window
in case you are there –
in case you have chased me
to hold me up,
kiss me or
kill me,
throw me on to the track.

The last time I left like this,
final exams over, the summer I went home
thin and exhausted, nothing to do but lounge in the
    garden
half asleep, or watch clouds,

you sent letters and wrote about
how you stalked my shadow in the cloisters,
following the memory of our love into the grove
where I darted with the deer,
slipping into the trees.
Why was I hiding from you?
I pressed the paper to my mouth and breathed
in your hand.

You told me that I should come back,
and soon.

'You read too many novels,' Dad said,
mowing the lawn,
growing tired of my indolence.
He'd never complained about my books before.
'Isn't it time you got a job,
started to pay off those loans?
What do poets earn anyway, Em?'
I shrugged and yawned.

'Not sure. Not much.'

It didn't matter then, in the beginning, when I was hooked.
You were the book I'd never read
and now I'd begun, I wanted more.
Smug with love, I told everyone you were the one
and stopped answering my phone or texts,
messages, emails, thinking only of you thinking of me.

ᴗ

It flashes at me, almost obscene, the memory:
you here on this platform, waiting for a train
to deliver me into your life.

And the kiss.
It was all love. Your lips too sweet,
unbearable. Soft.

You carried my suitcase as we walked to your home,
you held my hand
and love ripped through me.

We became Tom and Emma and I began to say
*we* instead of *I*,
losing myself in us.

You taught me to swim in the river.
I didn't think about drowning, trusting myself to the water
    and
staring up at the sun, your hand in the small of my back.


Later, in bed, you read *The Faerie Queene* aloud and I
    laughed
and rode, triumphant, upon my sea-shouldering whale:
this was victory, I thought.


You cooked for me and your tastes became mine.
I wrapped my tongue around your food,
licked it from your fingers.


Wherever I was, I could smell you on my hands,
lick salt from my upper lip
and taste your sweat.


We slotted together and
I didn't notice my key stutter in the lock
as friends fell away;
I let them drop and only when the drains
overflowed
in autumn
and truth drifted into the house with the leaves and the
    wind and
Hannah, pregnant on the doorstep, furious and betrayed,
did I begin to feel the cold.


You said the marriage had been convenient,
the children a mistake.
I lay awake, wondering


and listening for the nightingale.


∽

The train begins to move and you have not come.
I unlock my phone,
delete your number
and photographs
where you flirt with immortality –
Atlas shouldered, caught in vivid light –
and with them the threat of memory.

Hardwired to see success as undeserved, unearned,
I have reprogrammed myself
to know my worth.

I will not miss you
                        or return
                                or look for you again

and if you erupt on to my pages,
an ink stain, spreading and spoiling and seeping,
there will be no more mythologizing.

I will tear you out and leave you somewhere
for someone else to throw away.

What else is there to say?

I open my bag, pick up my pen,
balance its precious weight and steady strength,
the impulse of hope it holds, despite you, despite all:

there is so much more
of me to come.

# ACKNOWLEDGEMENTS

Hugest and heartfelt thanks to:

My brilliant editor, Alice Youell, with whom it has been a complete joy to work. Thank you for everything, Alice.

My fabulous agents. Jessica Hare, you are such a wonder! I'm so grateful to you and Hilary Delamere for your continued support.

The Doubleday and Transworld team for the magic they have wrought in bringing *The Poet* to her readers.

Tabitha Pelly for being the most tremendous publicist and supporter of *The Poet*.

Bella Bosworth for copy-editing so magnificently and Kate Samano for eagle-eyed proofreading.

Holly Ovenden for the astonishingly beautiful cover.

My wonderful family – Reids and Barrys all. Special thanks and love to my mother. And Eve, Emily and Oliver, who read, gave excellent feedback, and approved.

Fellow writers and very dear friends, in particular Alexia, Amy, Diana, Juliette, Rachel, Helen, Anna and the SCBWI north-west gang.

Bella Pearson for her unwavering support and friendship.

My lovely and hilarious students, colleagues, and friends at Loreto Grammar School.

Dearest and best – Alistair, Eve and Scarlett.

And finally, the inimitable Charlotte Mew.

Louisa Reid graduated with a degree in English from Oxford University before training as an English teacher at Cambridge. She now lives and teaches near Manchester. Louisa is the author of four novels for young adults; *Black Heart Blue* and *Gloves Off* were both nominated for the CILIP Carnegie Medal. *The Poet* is her debut for adults.